Going Home

All the best on your horse journies

[signature]

GOING 🐎 HOME
TERRY R.A. EISSFELDT

TATE PUBLISHING & *Enterprises*

 TATE PUBLISHING
& *Enterprises*

Going Home
Copyright © 2006 by Terry R. A. Eissfeldt. All rights reserved.
Visit www.tatepublishing.com for more information.

No part of this publication may be reproduced, stored in a retrieval system or transmitted in any way by any means, electronic, mechanical, photocopy, recording or otherwise without the prior permission of the author except as provided by USA copyright law.
Scripture quotations marked "Msg" are taken from The Message, Copyright © 1993, 1994, 1995, 1996, 2000, 2001, 2002. Used by permission of NavPress Publishing Group.

This novel is a work of fiction. Names, descriptions, and incidents included in the story are products of the author's imagination. Any resemblance to actual persons, and events is entirely coincidental.
This book is designed to provide accurate and authoritative information with regard to the subject matter covered. This information is given with the understanding that neither the author nor Tate Publishing, LLC is engaged in rendering legal, professional advice. Since the details of your situation are fact dependent, you should additionally seek the services of a competent professional.

Book design copyright © 2006 by Tate Publishing, LLC. All rights reserved.
Cover design by Rusty Eldred
Interior design by Brandon Wood

Published in the United States of America

ISBN: 1-5988653-9-0
06.10.23

For Mom

Thanks to my family and friends for the various ways you supported me during the writing of this novel.

Chapter One

The call came just as Grand and Thomas were signing a multi-million dollar loan. Not the best time to have tragedy strike like a latent cobra.

"Excuse me Ms. Taylor, you have a phone call."

"Take a message, Meg," Enid smiled an exasperated sigh to the two gentlemen.

"I'm sorry Ms. Taylor, but it's St. Joseph's hospital in Comox, on the Island. They insist on talking to you immediately." Meg stared like an animal caught in the headlights. She was a professional and knew the cost for this infraction on high finance etiquette.

"Excuse me, gentlemen, I will return shortly. Is there anything Meg can get for you? Coffee, latte, cappuccino?"

"No thank you, Ms. Taylor," Mr. Grand said curtly. "We don't have time for coffee."

Mr. Thomas simply looked bored, holding a three hundred dollar pen in a well-manicured hand.

Enid exited as gracefully as possible while a million

scenarios exploded in her head like the fireworks at New Year's.

"This is Enid Taylor," she stated as business-like as possible, with just the right amount of annoyance in her voice to let the caller know she was not impressed with the timing of their intrusion.

"Miss Taylor, this is Dr. Nichol, from St. Joseph's Hospital. I'm afraid there has been an accident."

Enid was hurled back in time by this simple phrase. Three years to be exact. Another call, another accident. Her father, her horse, her past life, had been erased.

Enid's face became ashen, her pulse raced, she couldn't get enough breath to reply. She just stood there with the phone held to her perfectly made-up face, framed by a chic, up-to-date cut of her auburn hair. The half-carat diamond stud in her right ear was being pressed into her scalp by the death grip with which she held the receiver.

"I… er, I… don't understand," finally escaped with the breath bursting to get out of her lungs.

"Your mother has sustained a broken femur from a horse kick she received this morning," continued Dr. Nichol. "She's fine. It's not life threatening. However, it was a severe break and requires a lengthy convalescence. The plaster hasn't even set and she thinks she'll be home in time for the afternoon lessons. You know how your mom is."

The relief that swelled over Enid was like a tidal wave. She was washed back into today. This wasn't a repeat of the horror from three years ago. As she exhaled further suppressed air from her lungs, she nearly fainted. She grabbed Meg's desk for support. Her breathing became more regulated, her pulse slowly returned to a normal rhythm. Her complexion however remained pasty.

Going Home

"Thank you for the phone call Dr. Nichol," Enid managed to say somewhat coherently. "I'll call her at lunch, but now I must return…"

"Enid, it's not that simple. You have to come home. Today."

"Dr. Nichol, don't be ridiculous, I'm sure Mally is more than capable of running things until Mom gets out of the hospital." Enid let the bitterness slip into her tone like the tide oozing up the shore.

"When was the last time you spoke to your mother, Enid?" asked Dr. Nichol, sounding far too fatherly for Enid's liking.

"I was home for her birthday in February." It came out too defensive, Enid knew. But once the tide starts to come up the shore, who can stop it?

"Mally is pregnant and quite ill. She hasn't been out to the farm once in the last month."

"Well, whoever my mother has hired to replace her I'm sure will do. I really must be going. I'm in the middle of an important closure." Enid put on the tone, posture, even the persona that got her to where she was in the bank: the youngest corporate loans officer in the history of the institution.

"Enid," Dr. Nichol barked, matching her stride for stride in changing pace. "There is no one else."

"Of course there is, Doctor, my mother has not single-handedly dealt with all the day to day chores since her back surgery. And, I repeat, I'm sure whoever is helping her is more than capable of dealing with a few days of feeding and cleaning the horses. Now I really must go." Enid returned the receiver to the cradle gently, purposefully.

"Is everything all right, Ms. Taylor?" queried Meg.

"There's been a slight acci... incident at home. My mom is in hospital but it is not life threatening. Therefore Meg, if Dr. Nichol, or the pope, or even, God forbid, my mother phones me in the next 15 minutes, for the sake of the bank, take a message!" Enid took a moment to retrieve her corporate loans officer image. Breathing a few deep breaths, she returned to Grand and Thomas.

Chapter Two

The answering machine flashed red like an angry stoplight in rush hour traffic. Enid had managed to bury the nagging guilt all day for not returning the mountain of messages on her desk. She knew when she got home she would have to pay the piper.

The first voice was a calm and professional Dr. Nichol.

"Please phone me, Enid. I know you have my home number. This is important. I would like to update you on your mother's progress."

The next voice was neither professional nor calm.

"Enid, what is going on? Dr. Nichol told me that you had more important things to attend to than Mom and her situation. What could possibly be more important? You know I can't leave Kelowna. We're headed into golf season at the resort. Not exactly a time I can take off." His voice softened, "Elizabeth is pregnant again, just, we wanted to wait a few more weeks to tell everyone."

Enid growled from somewhere deep in her gut, "Is there

something in the water? Why is everyone pregnant all of a sudden?"

"Phone me!" her brother yelled.

Enid pushed the next button with a resolve reserved for inmates on death row.

"Enid, it's Mally. Look, I know we haven't exactly been on speaking terms for a while. But, I miss you. Especially now... I'm pregnant. Maybe that's why I'm so emotional. I've been really sick and had to quit working at Homestead Farms. Besides, I felt guilty drawing a wage under the circumstances. Look, phone me, or your mom if you'd rather not talk to me. My dad is always available to you too. There are some things you need to know, Enid. Well, um, bye."

The tears came unwelcome and unwanted. Enid didn't have the strength to hold them back, kind of like the tide.

Mally was a voice from her past life. The one she fled, the one that died on that horrid day.

Why did she go ahead and get married? How could she? She abandoned Enid when she needed her more than anyone. Enid needed her more than Tim did. The wedding could have been put on hold.

Tim, how they fought over him.

Why did they have to grow up? They were such good friends, the three of them. The Musketeers. An unchecked smile broke across Enid's face. Such fun they had on their ponies. Flying across the fields, chased by unseen enemies, everything from hungry carnivorous dinosaurs to aliens. Until the day in high school when the three became two: Mally and Tim. It wasn't so bad, really. Enid had Home Boy. He was her other half. But then he was taken from her. Home Boy and Dad, both on the same day. Enid shook

Going Home

herself, trying to dislodge the memories, good and bad, out of her mind.

Mally chose, she can live with it, Enid thought bitterly.

Enid pounded the button for the next unwanted intrusion into her new life.

The voice was weak, vulnerable, and helpless.

"Enid, honey, this is Mom. I'm afraid I'm in a bit of a pickle. Dr. Nichol is being, shall we say, blunt with me. I am, for once, taking his advice. It seems a break in the femur can be more complicated than most and my age doesn't sweeten the picture any. It has something to do with blood clots and risks of stroke. I don't know, I'm on quite a bit of morphine right now so I may not have it all straight. You should phone him. But one thing I do know..." Her mom groaned, and her weak voice cracked. "I'll lose the farm, the horses, everything if you don't come home and help me till I'm on my feet again. I know this is a lot to ask, E, but there's no one else I can turn to." The last part ended in a sob. "Please come home as soon as possible."

Raw emotions flew at Enid like branches in a fierce winter storm. Sympathy—Her mom was always capable, strong, and resilient to a fault. To hear her in a weakened state asking for help was new territory. Shock—How could the farm be in such a financial state that Mally felt guilty to draw a wage and mom feared losing everything without Enid's help? Anger—Why was God continuing to punish Enid and her family? What had they ever done to Him except serve Him, and follow Him?

Even after the tragedy that took her husband and the star horse in her barn, Meredith Taylor had not turned her back on God. Enid felt sick. How could one continue to

13

trust, follow, even love such a heartless Deity? And where was her mother's church family now?

Bitterness, her old friend, took over. Dark memories of unsolicited advice, uninvited hugs, unnecessary platitudes after the death of her father from her church family crept to the surface of her mind. They still rang hollow, untrue and fake.

A new thought interjected demanding attention. *Now He wants to mess up, steal away, and destroy your new life? Just what does God expect to accomplish by this continued assault on your very being? Does He think you would actually return to your former life? Return home? Return to horses? Return to church?*

A disgusted smirk shadowed Enid's face. *Yeah, right,* she thought, *if I go home it will be for mom. That's the only place my loyalties lie. I at least owe her that much. She spent a lot of time and money to hone the skills I have. The skills she needs. I can run the barn for a few weeks.* A forgotten warmth seeped from her belly up to her chest. It was dissipating the tension that bitterness and anger produce. It was the realization she was needed, that she alone could make a difference in a bad situation. Sure she got a sense of accomplishment every time she closed a deal, negotiated the optimum rate on a loan, ratified a few binding clauses to the company's advantage, but this feeling was in another league. With a strangely familiar sense of peace she dialed Dr. Nichol.

Chapter Three

It was an hour and a half ferry ride from Horseshoe Bay to Departure Bay. Enid needed this window of time to reflect on the whirlwind of activity that occupied the previous 24 hours. The bright sun on this mid-April Friday was unsuccessful in breaking through Enid's troubled thoughts. Today should have been spent basking in the glow of landing the largest corporate loan in her white-hot career but instead of celebration there was crisis and confusion. It was like the day that she received her A Pony Club rating. Her father wanted to be home in time for church the next morning, Enid wanted to stay and celebrate with her friends so Michael Taylor set off alone with Home Boy behind in the trailer. A heart attack in a semi coming the other way sealed it so they never made it. Once more the bitterness began to flow. Enid shut it down. She had little time to rehash the unchangeable. Time to move on to what awaited her at Homestead Farms.

The phone call to Dr. Nichol was sobering. The break

was bad. Her mom had endured a 4-hour surgery. There were six titanium pins in her leg. She would be in plaster for a week or so then a splint cast for 12 weeks. And that was only the beginning. There would be physiotherapy and the constant threat of blood clots that could result in a stroke. Enid agreed to come home but only to assess the situation and to put a plan into action.

The six-week leave of absence was easier to get than Enid had believed possible. It seems being the star loans officer had it privileges. The call to her brother was less successful. Mike was totally unreasonable. He thought Enid should leave her job indefinitely to take care of the situation while he was willing to do nothing but send flowers once a week. And Lucy, well, she was in Africa saving the world. What could she do? Enid sighed. You can't pick your family, so the saying goes.

She locked up her Crossfire. The sleek silver sport's car was Enid's pride and joy. She had purchased it 6 months ago with a bonus she had earned after landing a multi-million dollar loan with an international company. Smiling with the memory of success, she ascended the escalator to find food. Enid hated eating alone but the early departure time meant she left her condo in False Creek well before breakfast. She ordered BC Ferries' version of Eggs Benedict and sat in a corner with the morning paper in front of her. She immediately went to the puzzle page and started working the crossword.

"Excuse me, may I share the table with you? It seems that The Ferry Corporation is making a profit today."

Enid looked up into the deepest brown eyes she'd ever seen. They were almost black. Surrounding them was a

Going Home

comely face and short brown hair. Not rugged and chiseled, just friendly.

"Uh, sure, no problem." Enid's face flushed.

"My name is Jacob," he said, extending his hand.

Enid shook it as business-like as possible.

"I'm Enid."

"That's a unique name," Jacob stated, smiling.

"My mom's a bit of horse fanatic. I was named after the author of *National Velvet*, Enid Bagnold."

"Ah, horses, hay burners, the sport of kings. Definitely past their usefulness to society."

"Past their 'usefulness' to society?" fire rose in Enid's voice to match the flush in her cheeks. " How do you define 'usefulness'? Is not the simple pleasure of partnership, unconditional love, the care of another over oneself worth something?"

"Oops, I guess the apple doesn't fall too far from the tree. Sorry, didn't mean to upset you."

"Forget it," Enid managed a smile. "Actually, I'm not even involved in horses anymore. Please excuse the outburst. I obviously need more coffee. Oh, and by the way, Jacob is the name of the dog in *National Velvet*."

Jacob laughed. It sounded hearty, easy, and homey. "Okay, let's get on to something more interesting. What clue are you working on?"

They worked every puzzle in the paper with a comradeship Enid hadn't experienced since the days of The Musketeers. By the time the last word was deciphered in the Scrabble Grams, the boat was about to dock.

"I guess I better get down to my car."

"Yeah, it seems to be that time." Jacob looked her straight

in the eyes. "Thanks for sharing your seat in the dining room and your paper."

"No problem. I would not have gotten 'zootomy' without your help." Enid had difficulty holding his gaze. He seemed to be looking straight into the very heart of her. It was too intimate. "Well, bye," she held out her hand for another business-like shake.

Jacob took her lead and returned a business-like shake. "Bye."

Enid found her escalator and returned to her car. She leaned back into the black leather seat and let out a breath she didn't realize that she was holding. It wasn't that men hadn't given her attention before, but there seemed to be something deeper to Jacob. He reminded her of her father.

Chapter Four

Coming up the half mile drive into Homestead Farms Enid couldn't help humming *Country Roads*. It happened automatically. A memory muscle in her brain kicked in without consent. It was a tradition her father had started.

The Taylors had bought Homestead Farms the year after Mike Jr. was born. Meredith dreamed of being a stay-at-home-mom, yet wanted to continue teaching riding. When the riding school came up for sale it was perfect. A twelve-stall barn with run out paddocks attached, a 100 foot by 200 foot outdoor arena, a small cross-country school, a four-bedroom country Victorian house—all located on 10 well-drained and fertile acres. Six years ago, the Taylors had added an 80 foot by 200 foot indoor school with a heated tack room, office, viewing area and a wash rack.

The first of the familiar twinges of guilt began to swirl in Enid's stomach. The plan for the indoor was birthed out of her need to be training consistently all year. Pursuing her

A Pony Club rating was a full-time job. The riding standard was high. Her horse needed to be an all-round athlete, and Home Boy, by Lion King out of her mom's Homecoming Queen was just that. Not only was she training for her A rating, she was also bringing the young horses along for resale and teaching the local Pony Club lessons. Her whole life outside of school was lived in the barn. It was her's to run, manage, and take over when her dad retired. This would have freed her parents to fulfill their dream of traveling around the world, volunteering their time at various missions and orphanages. Her father would have retired from his orthodontics practice at the end of this year.

As she turned the last corner of the drive that led to the house, she swallowed hard. Her mother's usually well-kept garden hadn't been put to bed last fall. Enid hadn't noticed the garden in February, as it was covered in six inches of wet snow. By this time in mid-April, it should have been a sea of colors and fragrances. The white tulips, violet hyacinths and dancing daffodils were absent. Soggy brown clumps of foxgloves and lilies were all that was left from last summer's bounty.

Mally had only quit a month or so ago, why had Mom been too busy to garden last fall? With more questions added to yesterday's load, Enid walked into the empty, dark house.

The first thing that struck Enid was the sepulcher-like air. The usual homey smells of fresh bread and Mr. Clean were undetectable. Enid turned some lights on. There were no logs in the box. The wood stove stood in the corner with a blank look in its central eye. Enid entered the kitchen to fill the kettle.

"When circumstances crowd out the peace in your soul it's time for cocoa," Mom always said. Enid reached for her

Going Home

favorite mug. It was a large pottery mug her mother had bought on a trip to England. She found it in the small racing town of Middleton. Her dad had surprised Meredith with a trip to see the Grand National in their 25th anniversary year. They were in England for two weeks touring all the horsy places and then spent 10 days cruising the Mediterranean—the trip of a lifetime. There were supposed to be many such trips. Her dad was dead within the next nine months.

The shrill whistle of the kettle snapped Enid back to the here and now. She filled the mug with boiling water and stirred the hot chocolate powder to smooth creamy perfection. Breathing in the aroma gave Enid a much-needed boost to her morale. Mom was right, as usual. She took the hot drink and sat in her dad's old leather recliner. Sitting in the familiar surroundings and drinking hot cocoa, prompted waves to action in her pool of memories. Enid had many memories in this room: Christmas mornings, Easter egg hunts, and numerous Pony Club studying sessions. Besides her family, only one other person had spent as much time here with her.

Mally.

The call to the Lewes residence last night was as hard, if not harder, than Enid had imagined. She had successfully avoided Tim and Mally for so long she didn't realize the wounds she associated with them were still raw and festering.

Tim answered. That fact in itself was enough for Enid to regret ever entering the 10 digits.

"Hello," came his clear and always cheerful voice. How could one person continually be in a good mood?

"Hi, is Mally there?" Enid tried to sound rushed to keep any small talk at bay.

"Enid, its great to hear your voice. We've missed you. We're sorry to hear about your mom."

So much for the breakwater Enid tried to create. This was the very reason she had not contacted them. She just couldn't deal with their eternal optimism. Besides they knew her too well to pull anything over their eyes or ears.

"Thanks Tim. Is Mally there?" Enid repeated stonily.

"Sure, just a sec."

"Hello?" Mally's deep rich voice filled the fiber optics between them.

"Mally, it's Enid. Look I know you're not well but I was wondering if you could arrange for the horses to be looked after till tomorrow evening. I can't make it to Mom's till the late afternoon."

"Oh, Enid I'm so glad you're coming home!"

Enid had to quell the urge to shriek, "I'm not coming home!" Instead she continued, "I don't have the phone numbers of the pony clubbers. In fact I don't even know who is in the pony club anymore, let alone who would be responsible enough to take on the chores." The only reason Enid quit talking was because she needed to breathe.

"Sure, Enid, I can do that. I can't wait to see you."

"Thanks. Bye." Enid disconnected before Mally could respond. She knew it was rude but she just couldn't handle any more.

Taking another sip of hot chocolate, Enid looked at the time on the grandfather clock. It was just after noon. She had made good time even with stopping in Naniamo for groceries. The last thing she wanted was to be accosted in the neighborhood grocery store by some well-meaning member of the church.

Enid hadn't planned on being there so early but had

Going Home

opted for the first ferry when sleep escaped her grasp at four in the morning. The extra time would be well-served in filling up the wood box and unloading groceries. She could then have a look at the schedule her mom kept on the large calendar at her desk before the obligatory trip to the hospital. Enid's plan was to finalize the help needed as quickly as possible so as to minimize the time she would have to spend in the barn.

It wasn't until after the groceries were unloaded and Enid was preparing to go out to the woodshed that she missed the dog. Where was JR? How could she have forgotten about him? Mally didn't mention him, not that Enid had actually given her a chance. Enid searched through the house in all the usual places. Mom's bed, his little dog bed on the floor, which he had little use for, the chair beside the fireplace, they were all empty. With anxiety beginning to grow, Enid put on her rubber shoes called muckers, and a jean jacket and headed to the barn.

"JR! JR! Come here boy!" Enid shouted.

She power walked down the drive toward the barn. She saw the school ponies munching on hay outside in their runs. A girl's face popped out from behind the door.

"Can I help you?" she queried blinking her big blue eyes in Enid's direction. She was dressed in jeans, muckers, and a rain slicker. Her shoulder length brown hair was in twin braids. She looked to be about ten years old.

"I'm looking for JR. The Jack Russell, is he out here with you?"

"No, he's at the vet's," the girl said matter-of-factly.

"The vet's? Do you mean Dr. Brown's?" Enid was trying to keep panic from invading her voice. "What's wrong with him?"

23

"Nothing that I know of. Dr. Brown took him home yesterday after the ambulance took Mrs. Taylor to the hospital." The girl's baby blues lit up. "Did you hear what happened?" She inhaled a vast amount of air, readying herself for an epic story when a woman appeared out of the arena.

"Ada, that will be all. I'm sure Miss Taylor already knows." She turned her face to Enid. It was obvious where Ada got her eyes. The woman was in her early 30's. She was about Enid's height and looked athletic. She extended her hand. "Hi, I'm Ede, Ede Larke. I'm the DC for the Pony Club. I recognize you from all the pictures in the club's album. It's an honor to meet you. You're an inspiration to all the members."

Enid was taken aback—her, an inspiration? How could that be? Sure she'd achieved her A rating but what had she done with it?

"It's nice to meet you and thanks for helping out." Enid shook her hand. "Actually, I don't really know what happened yesterday except that my mom has had surgery and will be out of commission for a while."

"Can I tell her Mom, please?" Ada's hands were clasped together in a prayer-like grip.

"Well, okay, but don't exaggerate." Ede smiled indulgently at her daughter.

Ada began the great intake of air when she caught the look in her mom's eye. Stopped in mid-breath she began the tale of woe.

"Well, I was here cause the vet came to see my pony, Mr. Big. He's brown." Her mom cleared her throat conspicuously. Ada looked at her and rolled her eyes. "I mean dark bay." Ede tried to hide a smirk.

"Anyway, Mr. Big, though he isn't really big cause he's

Going Home

a pony, had a sore ankle." Ede raised her eyebrows at Ada. Again the eyes went for a roll. " I mean fetlock. So Dr. Brown was picking it up and holding it for such a long time that Mr. Big got tired. My mom was holding Mr. Big's lead rope and Mrs. Taylor was standing beside Dr. Brown, when all of a sudden Mr. Big pulled away from Dr. Brown and did a capri… capri… what's it called, Mom?" Ada looked at her mom impatiently.

"Capriole," Ede replied.

"Yeah!" Ada exclaimed. "A capriole. It's when a horse rears up and then leaps into the air kicking out his feet. The Lippizans do it. Have you ever seen the Lippazaner stallions? I have. We went to the PNE last year and they were there and…"

"Ada, I'm sure Miss Taylor knows what a capriole is." She turned to Enid, "It happened so fast. He reared up, pulled back and leapt into the air. I'm afraid your mom was in the direct line of fire." Ede looked ashen, "I'm so sorry."

Enid was struck by the genuine sorrow in Ede's voice.

"Hey, it's okay. With horses you just never know. I'm sure it's not anyone's fault. Accidents happen." Enid stopped. Did she just say that? She took a deep breath. "Well, thank you both again for helping out. Maybe you could get me up to speed before you have to go, or do you have to get Ada back to school?"

"Oh, I'm home-schooled. Today we're studying," the inhale began, "Barn Management."

The two women looked at each other and laughed.

Enid bowed to Ada and said, "In that case you'd better show me what I need to know for this evening's chores."

The three of them went into the barn.

Chapter Five

Enid parked the Crossfire and turned off the purring engine. She took some time to gather her thoughts before she entered the confines of St. Joseph's. She leaned back into the black leather seat and put on her Josh Groban CD. As the familiar music filled the car, she let her thoughts present themselves.

Things were in order at Homestead Farms as far as the daily needs of the horses were concerned but there was nothing extra. The usual three month supply of grain and bedding was not stockpiled. There was enough for the next two weeks, if that. The hayloft was nearly empty, but being mid-April that was normal. Enid had no idea how many bales of hay were put up last summer. She was too busy with her new condo, her new car, and her new life to care about such mundane things. She would have to do a proper count at evening chores.

The lesson schedule consisted only of pony club students. There were no outside horses in for training and the four borders that had been there at Christmas were gone, replaced by only two new ones. About the only aspect of Homestead Farms that seemed thriving was Homecoming Queen. She was fat, healthy and rounded with her next foal due in mid-June.

Homecoming Queen had been an up and coming show jumper but at the age of four she nearly pulled her hoof off when it got caught under a root in a field. That was the end of her career as a riding horse and the launch of her great success as a broodmare. Ever since Enid was nine years old there had been a new foal to look forward to every other spring. She usually had a foal every two years because her mom insisted it took a year for her body to get back into shape after having a baby. Home Boy was born when Enid was 12. She was smitten from the time he poked his dark wet nose out of the sack. He was the first creature Enid had ever seen born. They were inseparable. The next three foals born were sold as yearlings. This hadn't bothered Enid as she was completely taken with Home Boy and didn't have eyes for any other horse. Homebody was born when Enid was 18 and she was ready to take on another foal. She convinced her parents to keep him. He was a well-started three-year-old when Enid left. She was showing him in the 3' Hunters and he won every class he entered. A rush of guilt shook Enid out of the reminiscence. Homebody hadn't been ridden in over a month. When she saw him at noon, his muscles were slack and his coat was dull. Home Hunter, the four-year-old gray gelding, and Homemaker, the three-year-old dark bay filly, looked soft and bored as well.

Homecoming Queen's last foal had died in December. He was the nicest colt ever born at Homestead Farms. Her mom had imported the Olympic Show Jumper gold medal

Going Home

winner's semen straight from Germany. Meredith had big plans for that boy. The Comox Valley was ready for some new blood in the horse breeding genetic pool. She was hoping to keep the colt as a stallion. Her dream slowly died with the colt. A strain of influenza gradually killed the little foal. The remaining vet bills were gradually killing Homestead Farms.

The Queen's rounded brown belly contained the full sibling to the dead colt. *Hope springs eternal,* Enid thought. She turned off the soothing baritone voice, opened the door of the sleek gray sports car, and headed for the hospital.

As Enid approached the nurse's desk, she spied Dr. Brown. The veterinarian, Mally's dad, had always occupied a special place in Enid's heart. He was warm, compassionate and funny. Although he had tried to comfort Enid after the loss of her father she had closed him out. She had closed everybody out.

"Enid," he came toward her and wrapped his strong arms around her before she could stick out her hand to ward him off. Enid stiffened. Dr. Brown softened his hug but didn't release her. It seemed an eternity but slowly, bit-by-bit, Enid began to relax into the safety offered in the firm, gentle and familiar grip. She could feel a lump beginning to form in the bottom of her throat. She was not going to have a melt down here.

"Thank you, Dr. Brown," she managed to squeak out. She also managed to sneak out of his embrace.

"I just came from Merry… I mean your mom's room. She's resting as much as she ever rests," he chuckled goodheartedly. Theodore Brown's namesake eyes twinkled when he smiled, they exploded in flashing bright lights when he chuckled and the fireworks that gave a show in an all out belly laugh was worth telling a good joke for. Enid had known Dr. Brown her whole life and seeing him now gave her strength deep in her bones that she didn't realize was missing.

"Did you hear that I'm going to be a grandpa?"

"Uh, yes, my mom told me." Mally's dad would be a fantastic grandpa. Her mom had died five years before from complications associated with a lifetime of diabetes.

"Your mom is in room 3B on the 4th floor. Would you like me to show you the way?"

"No thank you, Dr. Brown, I can find it. And thanks for helping out by taking JR. I'll come by and pick him up on my way home." Enid directed this at Dr. Brown as she began to walk toward the elevator. She turned to wave as she stepped inside. Dr. Brown was still standing where she left him, looking lovingly at her.

The doors closed encasing her in the metal box. Enid hated hospitals. She always felt so inadequate, so uncomfortable. She didn't know where to look, what to touch or what to say.

She found her mom's room and entered reluctantly. Not that she didn't want to see her mom, it was just that she didn't want to see all the contraptions attached to her mom that were holding her down like so many chains.

The room was as pleasant as a hospital room could be. Enid saw that her brother was true to his word in the form of a huge bouquet of carnations, lilies and baby's breath. There were three other bouquets: one from the church, one from the pony club and one from Dr. Brown. Enid realized that she had brought nothing for her mom, not even a card. Feeling guiltier than she did when she came in, she let her eyes drift to where her mom was resting.

Her mom's eyes were closed. Enid had entered as quietly

Going Home

as possible. Meredith didn't stir. Enid looked at the IV drip invading her mom's left hand. The pulse, respiration and blood pressure monitors bleeped and blipped erratically to Enid's untrained eye. She couldn't tell if the pattern was normal or wildly out of sync. *Yeah*, she thought, *inadequate, ignorant, and definitely out of my comfort zone.*

Enid shuffled her feet to rouse her mom without having to speak.

Meredith's eyes opened. She reached out her right hand to Enid. Enid stepped forward and took it.

"E, honey, I'm so glad to see you," her mom said quietly with a hint of a slur.

"Hey, Mom, how are you?" Enid felt stupid. What kind of a question was that?

"Well, I seem to be all tied up right now," Meredith Taylor forced a weak smile across her honey-colored complexion. Besides the IV and the monitors, Meredith's right leg was held up in a combination of pulleys and chains which reminded Enid of the gear the vet used to string up the horses for their annual teeth check.

"Are you in much pain, Mom?" Enid asked quietly.

"No, it's not too bad. They have all sorts of drugs pulsating into me through this thing." Meredith lifted her left hand.

"I hate to be on drugs but when you need them it's nice to know they are there. See this little button?" her mom held up what looked like the nurse call, but it was attached to the IV.

"I can push it to get morphine. Drugs on demand, yahoo." Meredith looked at Enid trying to coax a smile out of her youngest child.

"How are things at home?"

Enid gave in and smiled at her mom.

"Fine, all the horses are alive and kicking. Oh, I mean..."

Meredith giggled, "Hey, it hurts to laugh you know."

"I'm so sorry, what a stupid thing to say."

"E, it's the right thing to say. It's the funny thing to say. And besides laughter is the best medicine." Meredith squeezed Enid's hand.

"The work load isn't too much, it's just that the lessons have to keep going. They're paying the bills right now." Meredith looked into her daughter's green eyes.

"You will teach, Enid, won't you? It is just the pony clubbers. I haven't had time or energy for anyone else since the colt died."

"Mom, it's been a long time, I don't know." Enid looked away. "I'll find someone capable."

"E, I've been doing all the teaching because, well, I can't afford to pay anyone." Meredith swallowed hard, "I wasn't exaggerating when I told you I'm close to losing it all." A tear swelled at the corner of Meredith's eyes, overflowed and followed gravity down her cheek.

The angry outburst waiting behind Enid's teeth dissipated with the onslaught of salt water. Now wasn't the time to question the whys and wherefores of the financial situation. Now was the time to be there for her mom and to make it better, to do her part.

"Mom, don't worry. I'll make it work out. If I have to teach I'm sure I can handle it. But right now you need to rest and concentrate on getting better." Enid managed a confident smile and patted her mom's hand.

"You're more than capable, Enid, you're gifted."

"Mom, let's not go there right now, okay? I said I'll take

care of it and I will. Now you rest and I'm going to go rescue JR from the mean Dr. Brown."

Meredith brightened, "He's never forgiven me for leaving him there to be 'altered.'"

Both the Taylor women giggled.

Chapter Six

The Crossfire smoothly negotiated the route from St. Joseph's to the Brown Horse Vet Clinic. It was as if the car was on autopilot. Enid looked at the familiar surroundings. Besides having spent too many sleepovers to count here with Mally, she had worked at the clinic during the summer break all through high school. She had dreamed of being a vet one day but just couldn't buckle down to do the science. Riding was much more important.

Enid locked the car out of habit. There was no threat of theft here in the country. The Brown Horse Vet Clinic was located on the same property as Dr. Brown's house. It was quiet and removed from any main road. She entered the door to the waiting area and was greeted by a girl she didn't recognize.

"Hi, I'm Enid Taylor and I'm here to pick up my Jack Russell, JR."

"Yes, Miss Taylor, Dr. Brown said you would be by. He

would have liked to see you himself but was called out on an emergency. Colic."

The girl had short blonde hair, a nametag declaring her to be Susan, and a very professional manner. "I'll get JR for you. I'm sure he'll be happy to go. He acts as if he were in prison and we've practically given him the run of the place."

With a smile mixed with just the right amount of friendliness but not inappropriate familiarity, she went out the side door, which led to the kennels.

JR came bounding through the doors like a POW from a concentration camp. His smooth coat was mostly white with a dark head accented by black points over his eyes and the distinctive dark patch surrounding his cropped tail. As soon as he saw Enid, he started to whine and whimper and hold up his left front paw—his old car injury trophy.

Faker, thought Enid, but she couldn't deny him his rightful homage.

"Oh, you poor thing. Has the evil Dr. Brown locked you up and force-fed you doggie treats? Oh you're so hard done by."

Enid scratched him behind his ears and he started the famous leg twitch maneuver. Enid scooped him up in her arms.

"How much is it for his keep?" Enid asked getting out her credit card.

"Oh there's no charge. Dr. Brown left specific directions."

"Then thank you," Enid said. She hesitated then added, "Could you bring me up to date on the account for Homestead Farms?"

"Sure, it'll just take a sec to get it up on the computer. Here it is. The balance owing to date is $15,385.72."

Going Home

It took all of Enid's loan's officer trained control not to show a physical reaction. She deliberately slowed her breathing. It was worse, much worse than she had expected.

"When was the last time Dr. Brown was out on a call for Homestead Farms?" Enid asked politely.

"At the beginning of the month. He gave Homecoming Queen her last Rhino shot and did a check-up."

A broodmare needs regular shots of the Rhinopneumonitis vaccine during pregnancy to keep the virus at bay. If infected, the mare could automatically abort the unborn foal.

"Has Dr. Brown done the annual teeth floating and spring shots on the school ponies or the young horses?" Enid inquired neutrally.

"No, the school ponies are scheduled for this Wednesday and the young horses the first Wednesday of May," Susan informed her professionally.

"Thank you for all your help," Enid said. That would be at least another couple of thousand by the time the last tooth was filed.

In a bit of shock, Enid turned to go and grabbed the door handle. It wouldn't turn. JR started barking and Enid looked up. On the other side of the door Enid saw a mountain of boxes obliterating any view through the window. She let go of the door handle and it flew open away from her. The mountain of boxes jerked backwards and the top row fell to the ground revealing a shock of dark hair and a pair of unforgettable dark brown eyes.

"Jacob?"

"Enid?"

"What are you doing here?" they exclaimed at the same time.

"I work here," Jacob said as he picked up the fallen load.

"You deliver veterinary supplies in the Comox Valley?" Enid asked.

"No, I work here. I'm a vet. I just graduated from the University of Guelph, in Ontario." Jacob successfully put all the boxes down on the counter.

"Uncle Ted offered me a position I couldn't refuse."

"Dr. Brown is your uncle?" Enid was flabbergasted. JR was tired of being held and not impressed about being demoted to second place in the attention department. He yelped and squirmed out of Enid's arms.

"JR, come back here." Enid yelled. The terrier raced outside and proceeded to the kennel area to bark his freedom cry at all the poor inmates left in confinement.

"What about you, Enid of *National Velvet* fame?" asked Jacob. "Of all the vet clinics in all the towns in all the countries and you walk into mine," he added in Bogey style. "Not mine actually, my uncle's." He smiled.

"I grew up here. I actually worked here all through high school. In fact some pictures used to be," Enid looked behind the desk, "right there." She pointed at a 5x7 photo of a girl on a bay horse jumping into the water jump at Michael Lake and another one of her, Mally, Tim and Bekah showing off their Team First Place ribbons from a Pony Club rally.

"Oh, that's you? My Uncle, Mally and Tim all called you E."

"That's my nickname."

A cacophony of barking and yelping exploded from the back of the practice. JR came tearing back into the front office followed by a melee of dogs, big and small.

Going Home

"JR!" Enid shouted. "I forgot he's able to open the latches. I'm sorry."

Jacob closed the front door containing the escapees.

"No harm done," said Jacob goodheartedly catching a small Westie in one arm and grabbing the collar of a blue merle collie with the other.

Susan cornered the Golden Retriever and the Shitzu while Enid unsuccessfully chased JR around and around until she cornered him behind the desk. Scooping him up she joked, "I think our work here is done." JR joined in with a series of barks as they headed for the door once more.

"I guess I'll see you around," Jacob said.

"I'll put my money on Wednesday," Enid replied with a grin.

Chapter Seven

The chores went well that Friday night and Saturday morning. The rhythm of horses and their needs was long established in Enid's DNA and she unconsciously slipped into the life she had run from.

The school ponies were the same as when Enid left. There was Davy Crocket, the 25-year-old pinto that Enid had literally cut her teeth on. He was the smallest of the bunch at just over 52 inches at his withers, or 13 hands high. Each hand is measured as 4 inches. His partner in crime was Jesse James, a 14 hh, 20-year-old pinto pony. Wild Bill, a bay Thoroughbred Arabian cross gelding was the next oldest at 18 years. He stood a decent 15.2 hh. The tallest of the gang was Doc Holliday at 15.3 hh. He was a 15-year-old Cleveland Bay. Annie Oakley, also 15 years old, was the only girl in the band and stood 14.2 hh. She was a lovely rose gray Arabian mare.

They all nickered welcomingly each time the barn door opened in hopes that some unsuspecting new student had come to take pity on them in their starving states. In truth they were all round, glossy and in good health.

She had been home in February, at Christmas and Thanksgiving but the last time she had come down to the barn was about a year ago to see Homecoming Queen's new prince.

He had been spectacular even in a neonate condition. The bone structure, intelligent eye, confirmation and refined chiseled head spoke volumes of his future status in the world of Show Jumping. Enid had been stirred into thoughts of partnering with her mom in his future but once she had returned to Vancouver she quickly erased such nonsense from her mind. She didn't have the time, money or capacity to risk in such a venture. When he got sick in September and was dead by December, Enid knew she had made the right choice to stay away from entertaining such dreams.

The infamous Mr. Big was indeed small. He stood at 13.1 hh, was a registered gray Welsh pony and was seven years old according to his pony club approved stall identification chart. Enid didn't like him from the start. There was something sinister just under the surface that Enid instinctively sensed. At first she put it down to the rightful resentment she felt towards the pony because of his part in the accident. On Saturday morning, however, when he pinned his ears at her, she began to suspect that he was not a good pony for a sweet kid like Ada.

The other border was a 12-year-old quarter horse simply named Joe. He was a stocky 15.1 hh and wore a deep rich chestnut colored coat. Unlike Mr. Big, Enid immediately fell in love with his big bright kind brown eyes. Both Mr. Big and Joe were fat and healthy.

The Young Guns, as the horses in training were always

Going Home

called, looked the worst of the lot. They were not under-fed or abused in any way but it was obvious to Enid's trained eye that they were only being maintained. There was no work schedule for them and their manes and coats were left to cope with the changing season on their own. Homebody was a dull brown instead of a shiny bay, Home Hunter's gray coat was stained with dirt and manure, and Homemaker's black mane was full of knots. Of all the facts facing Enid squarely, including the bank statements, the condition of the Young Guns told her the most. Her mom's time and energy were stretched too thin or she had lost any drive to carry on. There seemed to be no reserves left in the bank or in the heart of Meredith Taylor for the future.

By mid-morning Saturday, Enid had put together a plan for the week. She had called Ede Larke and arranged a meeting with her for that afternoon. Enid wanted to see where the Pony Club was at with their yearly calendar of events, as well as discuss the resources available to her within the club to cover riding and Stable Management lessons.

As Enid was enjoying a cup of coffee in the big country kitchen, JR started to bark and scratch at the back door. A knock quickly followed and Enid opened the door to a pleasant looking woman in her fifties.

"Hi, I'm Leonora Tasky, I own Joe."

"Hi, I'm Enid. It's nice to meet you. You have a lovely horse," Enid said. She felt instantly at home with Leonora, as if she was a long lost aunt. *That's it*, Enid thought, *she reminds me of my mom. The same laugh lines, the same twinkle in her eye, and the same sense of peace around her.*

"It's nice to finally meet you, Enid," Leonora said kindly, "I've heard so much about you."

"Well, please don't believe everything my mom says!" Enid laughed.

"I've just come from the hospital. She looks as well as could be expected."

"Yes, I talked to her this morning. She had a good night and is anxious to get out of there."

"She's a bit impatient but they're not going to release her for at least a couple of days," Leonora added.

"Dr. Nichol phoned and warned me not to let Mom talk me into springing her from jail quite yet." Enid continued more seriously, "With the facts he presented to me about femur breaks and the complications that can occur he didn't have too hard a time convincing me. Anyway, I told him I have up to six weeks leave of absence."

"Oh, I'm glad you're going to be around. Joe and I don't have any great plans but we were hoping to do the 2'6" Hunter Division this year in the Island Circuit. I would love to take lessons from someone as qualified as you, Enid. Do you think you could fit me in?"

"Well, I wasn't planning on doing much teaching. I've been out of it for a while. There are a lot of good instructors around. Have you tried them?" Enid said kindly but firmly. She didn't want to sound rude.

"Most of them are pretty full and can't accommodate my erratic schedule. I'm self-employed. You wouldn't mind helping out if your not too busy would you? I'd gladly pay the going rate."

"No, of course not." Enid conceded.

"Good, how about in 15 minutes? I'll go get Joe tacked up and meet you in the outdoor arena." Leonora flashed an infectious smile and turned to go before Enid could reply. While Leonora jaunted down the path back to the barn,

Going Home

Enid was left gaping at the kitchen door. *What just happened? I'm giving a lesson? In 15 minutes?*

Enid slowly closed the door and looked around the kitchen as if the lesson fairy was going to appear any moment and give her an outline for mature riders on sweet quarter horses. Enid started to slow her breathing, an impulse from years of entering stressful situations. She had taken a course on sports psychology in grade eleven and it improved her ability to remember jumper courses and to stick to the game plan without falling into the trap of reacting out of fear and panic. She marched into the office/study and quickly found her old pony club binder. She had hundreds of lesson plans in there from over the years. Her first experience teaching riding took place when she was fourteen years old. She had achieved her C2 rating and her mom had implemented her into the pony club lesson schedule along with the other C2's—Mally, Tim, Bekah, and Olivia. The five of them eventually took over all the teaching duties of the D's for riding and stable management. They were a proud club at the end of that year when the D's had not only won Quiz Rally but also placed 2nd in the Team Rally and 1st and 3rd in the Jumping Dressage Championships at the end of the season.

She found the lesson plans for beginning jumpers and headed up to her room to change into breeches and a sweater. The etiquette of being an instructor kicked in and for her to show up in the arena without breeches was as likely as the Queen of England showing up at the Ascot races without a hat.

As Enid opened her drawer to find riding pants, she was aware that the last time she had worn them was the day her dad and Home Boy drove away to their date with death.

Three years had passed. Why couldn't Enid get past the pain? She shoved all the panic down deep into her belly and pulled on a pair of dark green breeches. They felt dependable, like an old friend. She went to the back door and found her old paddock boots, polished and ready to put on. Her mom probably wore the boots. They shared the same shoe size. Enid followed the path to the barn area and found Leonora and Joe calmly walking around the ring.

"He walks out nicely. He has more freedom in his shoulder than I first thought," Enid noticed.

"He's actually about 5/8 thoroughbred," Leonora said. "But thank the good Lord he is all quiet cow pony in his brain." She affectionately patted his glossy neck.

"Well, let's see what you two know."

Enid put them through their paces for the next 30 minutes and was pleased to discover that Leonora was a competent rider and Joe was a good pupil who was willing to work.

"Thank you, Enid. I learned so much, like how out of shape I am. I thought I had found all my riding muscles. Guess not," Leonora moaned.

"I had fun too. Joe's so willing, aren't you boy?" Enid rubbed the gelding between the eyes. Joe closed his brown eyes and lowered his head leaning into the scratch.

"He'll be your friend for life now," Leonora stated.

"Good, at least I'll have one of the boarders on my side," Enid mused.

"Oh, are you having problems with Mr. Big already? I was hoping he would cut you some slack on your first full day on the job."

"So it's not just me? I was feeling guilty about not

Going Home

liking him. I thought it was pent up rage for what he did to Mom."

"Unfortunately, that wasn't the first incident. He broke Ada's arm the first week they owned him. It was excused because he was in a new home with a new owner and Ada didn't exactly listen to the instructions your mom gave her."

Enid began to understand where the depth of sorrow in Ede's voice had come from.

"How long have they been here?" Enid asked calmly.

"Let's see, I came in the middle of January and they came February 14th, Valentine's Day."

"So how did Ada break her arm?"

"The second day they were here Ada went to get the pony out of his stall while Ede was still parking the car. Meredith was teaching in the outdoor and stopped the lesson to ask Ada to come over and wait until her mom arrived before she went to the stall. Ada appeared not to have heard and went ahead. As she opened the stall door the pony spun around and kicked out. Luckily Ada put her arms up instinctively. He would have kicked her in the head if she hadn't. It was only a green stick fracture so she was out of the cast in less than three weeks."

Enid found herself seething with anger. She had no tolerance for dangerous ponies. Neither did her mom.

"What did my mother do?"

"She put down some pretty strict rules for the Larkes. Ada isn't allowed to open the pony's door without supervision. She's to put on her helmet before she does anything with the pony. And Mr. Big was put on a three-month probation. If your mom felt the pony was dangerous they were to sell him and find a replacement with your mom's approval or move." Leonora spoke with care and sympathy, more than Enid felt.

"Mrs. Larke agreed to everything wholeheartedly, even though it would be very hard on Ada. Of course, Ada is just a little girl in love with her pony. She can't see anything wrong with him."

Enid did have sympathy with Ada and resolved to help them out in any way possible. She was now looking forward to her meeting with Ede more than ever.

Chapter Eight

Sunday morning broke warm and bright. Spring was serious about taking over from where Winter left off. Enid enjoyed a solid, deep sleep. She couldn't remember the last time she had slept for eight hours straight without interruption. She concluded that it must be from fresh air and exercise. Even though she worked out regularly at a gym, it was a poor substitute for the great outdoors and honest hard work.

Her meeting with Ede had gone extremely well. Ede was a conscientious and knowledgeable horsewoman. She had ridden as a teenager in the Four H program. She recognized the potential danger that Mr. Big presented and valued Ada's safety above any tears she would cry over Mr. Big's departure. Enid had promised to evaluate Mr. Big for them and to implement a plan of action. On Tuesday Enid and Ede would talk and then Ada would be advised of the plan later in the day.

Ede had filled Enid in on the state of the Merville Pony

Club. There were 16 members. Five untested members aged 6- to 8-years-old, four D's aged 8- to 10-years old, two D-1's each aged ten years old and five D-2's aged 10- to 13-years old. When Enid asked where the C's were, Ede explained that it was getting harder to keep kids interested past the D level. Because they had so much available to them for activities, not many parents or teens were willing to commit the time and money to continue into the C level. Most of the serious riders were specializing by the time they were in their teens and pony club requires a horse trained in dressage, show jumping and cross country jumping. Enid sighed, she had been very blessed to have had the opportunities and the horses available to her to achieve the coveted A rating.

With no C level members in the club, it became evident that the instruction would fall mostly on her. Ede and a few other parents were capable of teaching some of the stable management but Enid would be solely responsible for the riding lessons.

The pony club lessons were on Tuesdays and Thursdays. Tuesday saw the E and D level riders and Thursday hosted the D1 and D2 members. Enid had some catching up to do. She needed to review the requirements for testing.

The E, or untested, level was quite straightforward. In order to pass on to the D level the riders needed to be able to safely catch their pony, put on its halter, lead them and tie them up. They were required to do a simple grooming and be able to help with the saddling. They needed to be able to ride independently at the walk and trot and be able to keep the pony on the rail, or the outside edge, of the riding arena. The step up to the D1 level required greater knowledge of horse care, the ability to put the saddle and bridle on, known as tacking up, and to be able to canter and jump small

Going Home

obstacles. Similarly, to pass onto the D2 level an increase in the knowledge of horse care and riding ability needed to be demonstrated. The current D2 members had the biggest challenge to pass onto the C levels. The skill and knowledge required of both horse and rider increased dramatically.

Quiz Rally was a day dedicated to the knowledge of horsemanship. There was a written test, identification tables and various games to challenge the Pony Club members from all across the BC and Islands District. It was being hosted by the Parksville club and was a mere two weeks away. The Merville Pony Club was sending five teams of three members each. Hillary Daniels, a 13-year-old D2, would not be attending.

Enid had given Ede some old quiz rally tests and different ideas of how to prepare the teams. Ede had agreed to coach the two junior teams, which left Enid in charge of the three remaining teams. She picked Saturday morning as the time she would donate to Quiz Rally Reviews. According to Ede, most of the pony clubbers were free Saturdays. Enid would be seeing them all on Tuesday and Thursday so would confirm with them then.

As she entered the barn, the first thing Enid saw was a fresh pile of manure in the aisle. It was still steaming. Looking up she saw a bay face broken up by a white stripe down the middle looking back at her. Homebody stood in the middle of the aisle, acting as innocent as possible.

"How in the world did you get out of your stall?" Enid scolded the big gelding. She noticed that he had removed every halter and lead rope from the stall doors and dumped them on the ground.

She quietly walked up to the gelding and began to rub the white stripe rhythmically up and down. Homebody nodded in time with Enid's fingers. She left him standing there and proceeded to the feed room. She was relieved to see that it was secure and Homebody was in no danger of colic from overeating grain. She entered the feed room and put some grain in a tin can. Shaking it, she walked calmly into Homebody's stall. He complied with the request and meandered back into confinement.

Men, thought Enid, *they are truly ruled by their stomachs.*

The best conclusion that Enid could come up with was that Homebody rubbed against his door with his hindquarters and somehow maneuvered the locking mechanism to open. Whether it was an accident or some sort of trick, Enid was clueless. She would have to remember to ask her mom.

With Homebody safe and sound back behind a closed door, Enid finished feeding the hungry equines. When she came to Mr. Big's stall, she entered with a carrot. He came and calmly took a treat, proving Enid's theory about men and their stomachs. She put his halter on and tied him up near his feed bucket. She tied up a full hay net and then put his grain in his bucket. Enid was pleased that she had successfully fed him without incident. Little did the gelding know he would remain tied up for a few hours.

Enid removed the manure from each stall and swept the aisle. She secured the feed room door and then left the horses and ponies to enjoy their breakfast. The clock read 8:00 a.m. by the time Enid returned to the warmth of the kitchen and to her own breakfast.

"Lazy bum," she directed at JR as he continued snoozing by the fire Enid had made an hour ago. "I thought you were supposed to be my companion and accompany me as I do the chores," Enid teased. She filled her mug with coffee and sat beside the Jack Russell, scratching him behind his ears.

Going Home

The phone rang out cheerfully. Enid reached it before the second ring.

"Good morning," she stated.

"Hi, this is Jacob," the friendly voice replied.

"Hi, Jacob," Enid returned.

"My uncle told me that you attend the same church and I was wondering if you were going this morning."

Enid was taken aback. She hadn't entertained even a whisper of a thought about church this morning. It was bad enough at Christmas surrounded by her family with Mike and Elizabeth's children acting as a great diversion of any and all attention, but to go in there, all alone, without even her mother? She thought not.

"Oh, no, I couldn't possibly," Enid tried to sound light. "What with the chores and going to see my mom, I'm sure I can't fit it in." Enid hoped it sounded legitimate.

"If I picked you up and we slipped in late and left early would you come? I would love to meet your mom. I could have you to the hospital before 12:15 if we timed it right." Jacob sounded so convincing, like he was inviting her to some covert operation.

"Is your uncle making you go? Misery loves company so I here," Enid quipped.

"No, no, I mean I want to go. It's just that, well, I don't want to go in there alone with Uncle Ted. I hate being the center of attention, that's all. I thought that if we went together we could divide and conquer, so to speak."

"Oh, you want me to take the heat off you. Uh huh. Well, I don't know if I would be very successful at that. I'm sure you'll be way more interesting to the primarily female population than I," Enid teased into the phone.

"Wow has this gone all wrong," Jacob laughed. "I think I'll reboot."

With that the line went dead. Enid stared into the phone. Who was this guy? She hung up the receiver just in time for it to ring.

"Hello?"

"Good morning. This is Jacob Brown. We met the other day on the ferry. How is it going at Homestead Farms?" Enid could hear the stifled laugh, the tongue in cheek.

She couldn't help joining in with the laughter.

"Yes, Mr. Brown. I remember you. Everything is fine, thank you. And how is the new job going?" Enid could play the game.

"Very well, thank you." Jacob cleared his throat. "Would you care to join me this morning for a call on a local house of worship followed by a visit to the neighborhood hospital with time left over for a bowl of famous Broccoli Cheese Soup at Moxie's?"

Enid stopped breathing. Well, now or never. The whole diversionary tactic might just work.

"I would be glad to join you, Mr. Brown," Enid said gracefully.

"That's great. I'll be by to pick you up at 10:15."

"That sounds fine, see you then," with that Enid signed off before Jacob had a chance.

Enid looked at the grandfather clock. It was 8:30 a.m. She jogged back to the barn to untie Mr. Big. His lesson would have to be saved for another time.

∽

Standing in the shower, letting the warm water flow onto her head, down her neck and following the contours of her body to the drain, Enid had time to think about

Going Home

the people she would be seeing at church. She knew that her hesitancy had to do with the fact that she had never been good at hiding her feelings and right now she had no positive feelings toward God. She didn't want to be around the people who had hurt her, even if unintentionally. She was afraid someone would ask her how she was coping at home or with the barn chores. She was afraid that Mally and Tim would corner her and demand to have her over for dinner. She was afraid.

Jacob pulled into the driveway at 10:10 a.m. in a blue Dodge Dakota truck. Enid came out of the front door before he had time to get out of the driver's seat. She slipped comfortably into the passenger's seat.

"You're early," she said.

"So are you," he retorted.

They both smiled.

"Well, here goes nothing," Jacob said with a grin as he smoothly negotiated the long driveway back to the road.

They pulled into the church parking lot at 10:40 a.m. The service had started at 10:30 a.m. Music drifted out of the open front door, down the stairs and into the parking lot to greet the tardy pair.

"I love this song," Jacob said enthusiastically.

"Forever God is faithful, forever God is strong, forever God is with us, forever, forever," he sang along easily.

Enid knew the song. She used to love it when she believed it. How could she sing that now? It wasn't true for her. She began to regret she had ever let Jacob charm her into coming. Since she didn't have her own vehicle, she was stuck.

"Are you coming?" Jacob asked.

Enid realized she hadn't moved since getting out of the truck.

"Sure," she managed a quick smile. She walked toward the stairs a little behind Jacob.

As they entered the sanctuary, Mr. and Mrs. McGregor greeted them. They had been the official greeters since Enid could remember. She had been on the receiving end of countless Sunday morning hugs. Today was no exception. If Enid thought she would be able to sneak into the back of the church without anyone recognizing her, she quickly found out differently.

"Enid, honey," Mrs. McGregor enveloped Enid into her motherly embrace. Enid didn't stiffen as with Dr. Brown. She couldn't help but melt into such love.

"It's good to see you too, Mrs. McGregor," Enid said warmly.

"And who might you be, young man?" Mr. McGregor inquired of Jacob.

"I'm Jacob, Dr. Brown's nephew. I've come to help him in the vet practice." Jacob sincerely shook Mr. McGregor's extended hand.

"I believe there are a few seats in the second to last row on the left," Mr. McGregor pointed out.

"Thank you," Jacob said quietly. He guided her to the waiting seats.

Enid recognized quite a few people. She also noticed some new faces including Leonora. But the faces she dreaded, Mally and Tim, were noticeably missing from their usual spots—Mally at the keyboard and Tim on bass guitar. *She must be ill*, Enid thought. Mally never missed church. She and Tim were regular members of the worship team. *Well*,

Going Home

thought Enid, *thank God for small blessings*. He had spared her that uncomfortable moment at least.

The music changed to a more worshipful tone.

"I will bless the Lord, forever, I will trust Him at all times…"

The worship team sang with more than emotion. They believed what they sang. The congregation was entering into the experience with the musicians. The building seemed to be the outer shell infused with a life that was pulsating from all within. *All except me*, thought Enid. She didn't know this song. *It must be new*, she thought. That didn't surprise her. The church was always embracing new music from all over the world.

The chorus rang out, "You are my shield, my strength, my portion…"

Enid started to shake. The voice was calling her name: *Enid, just come, come to Me.* Enid closed her eyes, folded her arms over her chest and started to visualize the hayloft. She was counting bales. Somehow she made it through the song service. Pastor Dave came up while the music was playing softly.

"Thank you worship team. It's good to be reminded that our God is a good God no matter what the circumstances this life has to throw at us. He indeed is forever faithful, a present help in our time of need. Join with me in prayer." He lifted his arms to heaven and said, "Lord, Jesus, we come to you as your children. We thank you that you're faithful, a strong tower into which we can run in times of need. We bring before your throne of Grace this morning our sister, Meredith. We ask you, Lord, to strengthen her, encourage her, whisper to her even now where she lays in the hospital your great love for her. Giver her rest Lord and heal her body in your name, Amen."

"Amen," Jacob agreed.

Enid looked at him. *He must be a Christian or he's just putting on a show for me*, she thought. Then he looked her in the eyes, took her hand in his and said, "Amen."

She looked back at him blankly. She couldn't say it. She looked away but he still squeezed her hand like an old friend before releasing it.

Pastor Dave continued.

"It's great to see you all this morning, and it's my privilege to welcome home Enid Taylor who has come back to help her mom. Welcome home, Enid," He looked straight at her warmly. Familiar faces turned to her smiling, some waved, some clapped. She could only hold the pastor's gaze for a moment.

"As well, we welcome Jacob Brown who has moved to our community from Ontario to work with Dr. Ted at the vet practice. Welcome Jacob, won't you stand so we can all see you?"

To Enid's astonishment Jacob confidently stood up.

"It's good to be here among you. I feel right at home already and am looking forward to meeting you all." He sat down.

Enid stared at him wondering again, *Who is this guy?*

He smiled at her, "I met Pastor Dave and his wife Carol yesterday. Mally and Tim invited Uncle Ted and I over for dinner last night. Pastor and his wife were there as well. They're really great. You're so lucky to have grown up with such a great church family."

Pastor Dave opened his Bible and read. However hard she tried, Enid could not shut out the Word of God. Her

Going Home

father had loved reading the Word to his family. He instilled in each one a respect for it, if not a love.

"Please turn to the letter to the Ephesians chapter four starting at verse 26. I'm reading from The Message Bible. 'Go ahead and be angry. You do well to be angry—but don't use your anger as fuel for revenge. And don't stay angry. Don't go to bed angry. Don't give the devil that kind of foothold in your life.' And jumping down to verse 30: 'Don't grieve God. Don't break his heart. His Holy Spirit, moving and breathing in you, is the most intimate part of your life, making you fit for himself. Don't take such a gift for granted.'"

Enid felt searing pain cut through her heart. She had read Ephesians many times but never out of The Message Bible. It resounded deep in her like nothing had for a long time. Could she truly grieve God? Why not, He had grieved her. Enid clenched her jaw and mentally shut her ears.

Somehow Enid made it through the rest of the service by disconnecting herself from it. The same technique she used for disconnecting the fear and anxiety related with jumping horses she now incorporated into disconnecting with the hurt and confusion she felt within these walls.

True to his promise, Jacob motioned Enid that it was time to go just as Pastor Dave was calling the worship team up to close the service. With gratitude and relief Enid slipped out of the chair and followed Jacob to the still open front door. They could hear the worship team singing "You are my shield, my strength, my portion…"

"Shall we proceed to the hospital, my lady?" Jacob asked with an unexpected English intonation.

Enid appreciated his sensitivity and his wacky Brown family humor.

"The hospital, Jeeves, if you please," Enid replied in the best upper crust accent she could muster.

Chapter Nine

The twenty-minute drive to the hospital was quiet. Jacob drove, humming to himself and every once in a while smiled over at Enid. Enid slowly but surely relaxed and let the pain and confusion go back into the deep part of her that had been too often exposed these last few days.

Enid led the way up to her mom's room on the fourth floor. Even before they entered, Enid could hear her mom laughing. As they entered, it was obvious that Meredith was on the phone. She was just saying good-bye when Jacob and Enid appeared from behind the curtain.

"Thank you so much for calling, sweetie. I love you too. God bless." Meredith hung up the phone still laughing.

"That was Lucy. She was telling me the latest high jinx the kids were up to in the orphanage," Meredith looked from Enid to Jacob. "You must be Jacob. Ted has told me so much about you," Meredith offered her hand. Jacob grasped it tenderly.

"It's great to meet you, Mrs. Taylor. My uncle has told

me a lot about you as well," they smiled at each other like compatriots. Enid didn't get it.

"Mom, you're looking a hundred percent," Enid interjected breaking the eye lock. She hugged her mom affectionately. Her leg was no longer strung up like a duck in a Chinese grocery but was propped up with pillows. The monitors were thankfully absent with just the IV remaining like a stubborn leech attached to her hand.

"I see some progress has been made since yesterday," Enid noted with pride.

"Oh, yes, I'm coming right along," Meredith added with equal pride. "Hopefully I will be out of here in a few more days," she looked earnestly at Enid, "E, how are the babies?"

"Which ones?" Enid grinned in mock exasperation. "The school pony babies, the Young Guns or the biggest baby of them all carrying a baby?"

Meredith smiled broadly. "Let's start with the biggest baby and move on from there. A complete report, please."

Enid gave her mom an overview of how all the horses were doing. She even ventured into the Young Gun's lack of exercise and training.

"I just haven't had the time or the energy, and I suppose if I'm honest with myself, the desire to ride and train them. Mally was doing most of it for the last few years. I've made a lot of excuses, but laying here the last few days, certain things have popped into perspective. I'm pretty well finished with the full time horse game. I have other things I want to do with my life. I'm not getting any younger and time waits for no one," Meredith stopped speaking and simply looked deeply at Enid. She sensed the fertile silence develop into a full term pregnant pause, ripe with life yet undetermined.

Going Home

It seemed time stood still and even Jacob appeared to have stopped breathing.

"I've decided to sell out, E."

Enid's eyes were stuck on her mom's mouth. Did she just form those words and did they just exit up the throat, over the tongue, through the teeth and out the lips? Had Enid heard correctly?

"Everything?" she gasped.

"No, I could never sell Queenie. Cheryl would let me retire her at her place if I no longer had a place of my own."

Cheryl Gabriel was a long time friend of Meredith's. She had bred Homecoming Queen and stood most of the stallions that Meredith had bred to over the years including Lion King who was Home Boy and Homebody's sire.

"Not have a place of your own, you mean your selling the property too?" she couldn't stop the bit of a whine that entered her tone.

"The family we bought it off of recognized that they were done and we were the blessed family it came to. I recognize now that I'm done and I'm sure there's someone ready to start with the passion and energy I now lack," Meredith had the same old resolve in her voice that Enid had experienced growing up. It was the tone with the disclaimer "No discussion" at the end of it.

"This won't happen overnight, E, I have a lot of work to do to get the place ready for a realty sign but I've never kept things from you and I won't start now." She turned her gaze to the young man, "Jacob, how are things going at the practice with Ted?"

Jacob's smile broke the gloom that threatened to descend on the room bright with flowers.

"Fine," he stated simply. "The practice is larger than I thought. I can see why my Uncle was looking for a partner."

Meredith and Enid both looked surprised.

"A partner? I thought you were just working for your uncle?" Enid joined the conversation again as clarity returned to her shocked mind.

"Yes," Meredith added. "Ted never mentioned this to me."

"I guess it seems my uncle has been thinking of his future too, these last few days." Jacob glanced at Meredith. "He feels a change in the breeze and wants to go with it. There are other things he desires to do in his lifetime as well."

Meredith looked away. Her gaze seemed to fall on a certain bouquet of lilies.

"I suppose we are at that time in our lives," Meredith said wistfully.

"So how is Lucy, Mom?" Enid interrupted the swirling emotions in the room.

"Lucy is doing just fine. The orphanage is building on again and they hope to be able to accommodate 10 new children by September," Meredith said warmly.

"Lucy's in Ethiopia, is that right, Mrs. Taylor?"

"Yes, Jacob, in Addis Ababa."

"I was there two years ago with Vets Without Borders. It doesn't sound quite as significant as Doctors Without Borders, however, the people do rely on their animals for food and income. Just 10 chickens can make the difference between being destitute and starving or being able to feed your children and afford to send them to school." A passion rose in Jacob's voice that sounded similar to whenever Lucy spoke about Africa and the work she did there.

Lucy had entered nurse's training right out of high

Going Home

school and graduated the year Mike and Elizabeth's twins were born. She was working full time the year that her father died. After the anniversary of her father's death passed, Lucy announced that she was going to Hawaii to the University of the Nations with YWAM, an international missions organization, to be trained up for a position overseas working with children. One year ago, Lucy was assigned to the orphanage in Addis Ababa. Enid felt great sadness whenever she thought of Lucy. She had been extremely upset with Lucy's decision. Enid had thought they could share a condo together in Vancouver and go to plays together, to the ballet, the symphony. Do sister stuff. But Lucy was too otherworldly in her thinking.

"E, how can I spend my life on myself when someone is dying every three seconds around the world because of poverty?" Lucy was the first one to bring home strays or cry whenever the yearlings were sold. She played with dolls while Enid had played with horses. She completed pony club to C2 at her mother's insistence but was released after that to pursue her studies. She had the full course of Science and Math in high school and ate it up like Enid and Home Boy did a cross-country course. Meredith was always good about letting her children pursue their own passions.

"What did you think about Ethiopia, Jacob? I've never been there and only know what I see on TV or read in the paper. Is it really as devastated as it appears?" Meredith questioned.

"It's a totally different world. There's nothing to compare it to in Canada. It's a Muslim nation and so the flavor of the culture is intertwined in their religion. Every place in this world has its own beauty and its own scars. The people of Ethiopia, especially in the North, bear the scars," Jacob sighed. "I think that no matter how much one does for good, without the Lord despair would steal any joy. But we know that even a cup of cold water given in Jesus' name can have eternal repercussions."

"That's true, Jacob. And wise. I struggle not worrying about Lucy being in a hostile environment. Yet I know beyond a shadow of a doubt that she's in the center of God's will for her life. There really is no safer place to be. No matter what happens to our physical life, no one can snatch us out of the hand of God," Meredith looked with tender compassion on her youngest child. She knew the demons with which Enid was tormented—unbelief, doubt, anger, unforgiveness—all directed at God. These were all part of the grieving process one had to go through after such a senseless tragedy. Meredith had chosen to embrace the pain and let Christ, who bore all things for her, embrace her. It wasn't easy. It was hell. But she let people, even inadequate people, speak to her. At times she was surrounded with Job's counselors: good intentions mixed with ignorance and devoid of shared experience. However, Meredith, in her grief, extended to them the grace that Christ had extended to her. Free without judgment. She had learned this lesson well over the years working with both unruly horses and children. Enid didn't have the depth of perspective to carry her through and when she closed her heart to imperfect people, she stagnated in the natural grieving process trapping all the destructive messages from the pit of hell. She was deceived into thinking them to be her new reality. Meredith knew she could only continue to bring her daughter before the Throne of Grace in prayer, and to keep extending to her the love that rights all wrongs and frees all captives; the love that sent a much-loved son into the world to be killed.

Going Home

"Lucy sends her love, E, and her apologies for not being here with you to share the load."

"That's okay Mom, I'm finding muscles I'd forgotten I had." Enid tried to be lighthearted and to change the course of the conversation. "So I think I have a plan for Mr. Big."

She outlined the course of action she was going to take to her mom. Meredith was both pleased and supportive.

"You've read him right, I think, E. You also have the skills I don't possess to follow the plan through. Just be careful, honey. Use your horse sense and the buddy system."

Always the instructor, Enid thought without malice. "I promise, Mom. Who would come to our rescue if I was in the bed next to you?"

"I would try," Jacob chirped in, "but according to my uncle, the Taylor women are fairly self-sufficient," his brown eyes twinkled, matching his grin, "and stubborn."

Meredith and Enid put on shocked expressions.

"Us?" Enid said.

"Stubborn?" Meredith added.

"Never," they replied in unison.

The three of them broke into laughter.

"Well, you two have brightened my day. I guess I should kick you out so I can have my afternoon beauty sleep," Meredith gave an exaggerated yawn.

"We get the point," Enid said laughingly.

"Not that you need a beauty sleep, Mrs. Taylor," Jacob flirted.

"You're too kind, young man. Now off you go to lunch or whatever free people of the world do on a lovely spring afternoon. I must succumb to my imprisonment." With a bit of melodrama Meredith put her hand to her brow and fainted back on to her pillow.

"You're still the biggest drama queen of us all, Mom," Enid teased. She bent over and kissed her mom's forehead.

"Rest up and it won't be too long before I spring you from this place. I love you."

"I love you too, E. Thanks for coming," Meredith reached out to Jacob once more. "And thank you too, Jacob. It's been great to meet you."

Jacob warmly took the hand extended to him. "Take care Mrs. Taylor and I'll see you soon."

Enid left the room expecting a quiet lunch with Jacob.

They never made it.

Chapter Ten

As the elevator doors opened on the ground floor they revealed a distraught Tim Lewes.

"Tim, what are you doing here?" Enid reached out to him instinctively, recognizing deep pain and a tortured soul.

"E, oh, E. We've lost the baby," Tim groaned out in a voice not his own. He collided into Enid as she rushed toward him. As he stretched his arms around her, he let out a wail that rose from the deepest part of his being. Jacob encircled the both of them in his strong arms, giving support to otherwise lifeless limbs.

Enid was left speechless. There was nothing to say. The trio stood there blocking the path to the elevator until Tim's sobs subsided into whimpers and he could stand under his own power. Jacob released the tension of his embrace from bearing all their combined weights to a gentle hug easily escaped from. Tim stood up straight, breaking the chain of arms entangling them.

"I'm sorry," he choked out.

"There's nothing to be sorry for," Jacob said with tenderness. "Is there anything we can do for you?"

Tim looked at Jacob, aware of him for the first time. "Jacob, I'm so glad you're here," he gripped Jacob's hand as if his very life relied on it, "please call Dad Brown."

Tim's full eyes fixed on Enid. She felt his pain, she knew his pain, and more than that, she shared his pain.

"E, pray for Mally, she… she…" the dam broke open once more, "She lost a lot of blood. I just about lost her too."

Barely able to respond without falling apart herself, Enid merely managed a whispered "Yes."

"I've got to get back to Mally," he said desperately. The elevator opened as if in response to an unspoken command. Tim stepped into the empty chamber and the doors closed, cutting off the specter of death that accompanied him.

With all the remaining strength Enid had left, she dialed Dr. Brown. He hadn't returned from church yet, so Enid left a message.

A quiet sob escaped Enid's lips. Immediately she felt Jacob's strong arms encasing her. She leaned into the embrace thankfully.

"Please take me home," she sobbed.

Jacob literally carried her to his truck and gently helped her into the passenger seat. The drive home was quiet but not strained. A peace surrounded Enid in spite of her grief-stricken thoughts.

When they arrived at Homestead Farms, Jacob escorted Enid into the kitchen and proceeded to put the kettle on. Enid sat frozen on the rocker beside the woodstove. She was aware of Jacob's presence and was comforted by the fact that she didn't have to be alone. When the kettle boiled, Jacob

Going Home

searched out mugs and hot chocolate powder. He carried the steaming mugs to Enid and sat down in her dad's old recliner.

"So how much do you really know about me?" Enid asked stonily.

"I've known about you for quite a few years. Mally would always tell me tales of your adventures. I know that three years ago a lot more died than just your dad and your horse." Enid flashed an angry look at him.

"Don't talk about my dad or my…"

Jacob cut her off, "You don't have the market cornered on loss, Enid. Most people walking around have suffered great loss. Mally lost her mom five years ago and now her first child. Dr. Brown has lost his wife and now his first grandchild. Death is real, loss is real, pain is real but we don't have to be its prisoner." He put his mug down, got out of the recliner and knelt in front of the rocker. He cupped Enid's face gently so he could look her in the eyes.

"Not with the power of the cross at our disposal. Jesus paid it all, the ultimate sacrifice so we wouldn't have to be captives in the kingdom of darkness."

Tears streamed down Enid's face unhindered. She held his gaze. Deep down she knew he was right. It had just been so long. The anger, bitterness and unforgiveness that had forged a bond in her soul would require too much pain to separate. At least he didn't tell her to suck it up or that God's grace was sufficient. He spoke as one who had gone through loss and had come out the other side.

"How do you know?" she asked the question in all sincerity, hopefully.

"I do. I don't want to share my story with you quite yet, but I will. I promise."

She believed him. A wave of peace washed over her.

"Okay, I'll wait. I'm okay, really I am. I have the chores to do and my week to plan. I'll be all right. You should go and be there for your uncle and cousin." He wiped the tears away from her cheeks with his hands. Then he stood up.

"Enid, thank you for coming to church with me. And thank you for introducing me to your mom. How about a rain check for lunch? Wednesday, after I do the ponies?"

Enid walked him to the door.

"That would be fine, Jacob. Thank you for being here." She looked into the now familiar black pools his eyes were. He stepped forward and gave her a hug.

As she watched him drive away, she was struck by the warm feeling in her stomach. She couldn't remember the last time she had been hugged by so many people in one day. Her mom always said that everyone needed at least eight hugs a day just for maintenance and many more than that to heal from any pain. She had a lot of catching up to do.

Chapter Eleven

Monday morning dawned as bright and promising as the day before. After yesterday, Enid would put no stock in the sun. She rose out of bed to the familiar licks on her face from JR. He was only thinking of his own full bladder and empty stomach, not the romantic thoughts such as, "Man's best friend wakes sleeping mistress" that Enid had entertained as a small child.

She let the dog out and got on with her own morning routine. After making her bed and getting dressed in fawn breeches, a navy T-shirt and a navy hoodie, she put the coffee on and headed to the barn.

All the equines were in their stalls where they were supposed to be, including the Houdini impersonator Homebody. The ponies all nickered their welcome with the exception of Mr. Big who merely looked out his window with an impatient toss of his head as if to say, "Get on with it!"

Enid gave the horses their hay, leaving Mr. Big for last. Once more she entered with a carrot and won him over. She put his halter on and tied him up with a full hay net in front of him. Enid left him and repeated the same process with the grain. She swept the aisle and then returned to the kitchen for her coffee and toast.

Enid enjoyed a leisurely breakfast with her old pony club manuals in front of her. She mapped out lesson plans for the following day and after evaluating the riders tomorrow, she would make a month long plan.

Around 9:30 Enid headed back out to the barn. The horses were all done with their breakfast and were already basking in the spring sun out in the attached runs. Mr. Big was standing sedately staring at his empty hay net. Enid grinned to herself. She entered the stall and the pony pricked his ears forward, eager to be released from the confines of the rope. She rubbed him on his broad forehead and told him how clever he was. She left him once more and started to clean out the stalls. He kept his eye on her the whole 45 minutes it took her to complete the job. As each stall was cleaned, Enid would come in and visit Mr. Big and give him a rub or a scratch and tell him how lovely and clever he was. The pony ate up the attention. By the time Enid was finished the chores, Mr. Big nickered out a friendly greeting each time Enid passed by.

When the stalls were completed, Enid came back to Mr. Big, this time with his grooming caddy in hand. When he saw it he put his ears back and swished his tail. Enid immediately left his stall, taking the caddy with her. She turned her attention to the feed buckets instead and brought them to the wash rack to be cleaned. She ignored Mr. Big.

At first he tried to take no notice of Enid but his natural curiosity and herd instinct enticed him to start the nickering campaign of good will once more. When Enid

Going Home

had all 10 buckets scrubbed clean and drying out on a shelf she returned to Mr. Big. Once more she entered the stall with his grooming caddy. He didn't pin his ears back this time but neither did he look pleased to see her. Enid took it as a neutral attitude and arming herself with curry comb and body brush began the familiar routine of grooming. Mr. Big tried to stiffen his body from the rhythmic motion of Enid's experienced hands but his resolve didn't last long. Ten minutes into the session he was won over, forelock to tail. He started to lean into the deep massage Enid was applying to his wither area. With his head tilted and his neck stretched out he curled his lip in what can only be described as ecstasy. Enid was smiling satisfactorily. There was not a horse that ever came to live here that Enid had not won over. Mr. Big had met his match.

After the grooming was complete, down to oiling the hoofs, Enid released Mr. Big to his paddock. He didn't run off but rather, like a hostage who has fallen in love with his abductor, he waited until Enid had left his stall before he went out for the obligatory roll to put his coat back to the way he liked it. Enid walked up the path to the house with a distinct swagger added to her step.

She entered the kitchen just as she heard the answering machine clicking off. She reached for the play button to hear her mom's voice.

"Hi honey, it's Mom. Dr. Nichol has just told me that if all continues to go well, he'll release me Wednesday morning. I know that Dr. Brown, Dr. Jacob Brown, is due out there for the ponies, so if you don't mind Ted will come and get me from the hospital. But if you would rather come that's okay, just let me know. See you later this evening. Bye, love you."

The machine clicked off and Enid let the buried

suspicions rise to the surface of her thoughts. *Mom and Dr. Brown, hmm.* As the idea was floating in suspended animation in her mind, Enid let it settle in the compartment reserved for things to celebrate. As much as she loved her dad and grieved for his loss, she wasn't an adolescent. She would not let her bereavement stand in the way of her mom's future happiness or security.

After a lunch of chicken noodle soup and a grilled tomato sandwich, Enid phoned her mom's accountant to make an appointment for the following day. The offices of Midwell and Stephans had handled the Taylor books for over 20 years.

The friendly voice of Mrs. Harper answered with a pleasant, "Good morning, Midwell and Stephans Accountants, how may I help you?"

"Hello Mrs. Harper, this is Enid Taylor. I'm phoning to set up a meeting with Mr. Stephans for tomorrow, if possible."

"Yes, Enid, I can fit you in at 10:15 tomorrow morning. Would that suit you?"

"That's perfect, thank you. I'll see you tomorrow morning."

Enid felt confident that the meeting tomorrow would bring clarity for her mom's future and that of the farm.

Enid headed back out to the barn. A nervousness that hadn't been at the surface of her mind for three years accompanied her. She was going to ride. She didn't think that she would be nervous. She had never been a nervous rider. She'd only confronted swirling butterflies before a competition or a Pony Club test. Employing the breathing technique so familiar to her, she opened the tack room door.

Her tack trunk was sitting in its regular spot. For the

Going Home

first time since she had been home, she let her eyes rest on it, look at it. The trunk was dusted and oiled like a loved piece of furniture. She shouldn't be surprised. It was a gift for her 16th birthday, hand-made by her dad. How could she think her mom would let it sit in a corner and rot? Enid ran her hand lovingly over the locked lid. She recalled the treasure hunt her father had made her go on that birthday morning. He had made up clues that led from her room to the hayloft, back to the kitchen, then to the woodshed, and finally, back to her bedroom. There it sat gleaming a reflection from her father's loving eyes.

Enid automatically reached behind the left front wheel and found the key. She fit it in the lock and turned. As the tumblers released the mechanisms of the lock with a loud click, Enid released a sigh from deep within. The lid opened to reveal the wool blanket Home Boy had won the year he died in the 4'6" jumpers. Hesitantly at first, and then with a hunger she had suppressed for so long, she reached for the blanket. She squeezed it to her chest. Dropping her face into the blue wool she cried and screamed and wailed like some ancient mourner. The tears were hot against her face. She beat her breast with the blanket, shouting out all the rage and questions she had internalized for so long.

"Why? Why? Why did they have to die? I hate you God! I hate you for taking them! You ruined my life!"

She broke into deeper wails, inhuman to human ears. She cried till the tears were gone and the wails became moans. She could hear the beat of her own heart, strong against her ribs. She didn't open her eyes. She slowly became aware that she was sitting on top of the tack trunk. She couldn't recall closing it or sitting down. She lay on top of it with her legs curled up and her eyes still closed. She wrapped the wrinkled wool over her. She lay under it like a mummy, as still as death except for the regular rising and falling of her breath. As her breathing became normal and as her mind became sharpened to her surroundings, she heard the muted plodding of hoofs over sawdust. The horses were coming in from the runs, looking for their lunch hay.

Slowly Enid opened her eyes. She saw the blue canopy over her head and sighed. She felt a release from deep within her being. What was left was a cold, empty cavern in her soul. As she lifted the blanket from over her head, she was stepping out into unknown territory. She didn't know how to cope or manage her life without the knot of anger and rage in her belly. How did she go on with this cold emptiness? Why go on? What really mattered anyway?

She was jolted out of her funk with a loud metallic ringing. She leaped off the tack trunk, letting the blanket fall to the floor. Looking down the aisle, she saw Homebody's stall door jarring back and forward and then watched it swing open. She walked toward it and came face to face with the bay face and white stripe belonging to Homebody. He was just exiting his tiny kingdom. He stopped and looked at her expectantly.

"What do you want from me?" It came out full of bitterness and resentment.

The gelding backed away from Enid. She broke into tears she didn't know could still exist. They ran in a stream to her cheeks. She reached out her hand to touch the gelding on the shoulder.

"I'm so sorry boy," she said haltingly. "It's not you I'm mad at. Nothing is your fault."

Homebody pushed her with his brown nose insistently.

Going Home

She could not keep a smile from invading the territory of tears. "So you do want something from me after all."

The gelding pushed her chest again.

"You're bored, aren't you?"

Enid deliberately took five deep breaths as she scratched the gelding on the withers.

Decision time.

She left him, closing his door behind her. She went back to the tack room and opened her tack trunk. Holding her breath and clenching her jaw, she moved the pile of ribbons and found the brush box. Picking it up she returned to Homebody. He stood patiently for his halter to be put on. She tied him up and started her grooming routine. First his feet were picked out. He had well-shaped, strong black hoofs. She then picked up the currycomb. The dull loose hair came out in volumes. Working from head to tail, it took Enid a full twenty minutes before she felt that she had released Homebody from as much hair as she could. He stood rock-still, loving the massage. Enid reached for the dandy brush and once more started at the head and worked to his tail on both sides, brushing off the surface hair and dust that the currying had left. She then picked up the body brush and started to brush out his long dark mane. It took twenty minutes of hard work before she could brush through his once tangled mane and tail. She stepped back and looked at the tall gelding.

His head was large but not crude. It was well shaped with good breadth between the brown eyes. A flat nose led to generous nostrils and a soft muzzle. His neck was long with a good crest leading to well-developed withers, attached to a short back and loins. His croup was built for jumping. The depth of his hip was staggering. Enid could imagine the thrust power. Here was a horse designed to do a job. His cannon bones were short with strong tight tendons. The pastern and shoulder were at a lovely 45 degrees. He had matured into a beautiful horse.

Enid took a soft cloth and gave the gelding a final wipe. The tiniest shine came to the surface of the dark coat. With renewed vigor, she returned to the tack trunk and lovingly picked up her saddle. She had spent more time in this saddle during high school than at her desk, or so it seemed. Its tan leather was as smooth and supple as any Italian leather furniture. She found the matching girth and bridle. She carried the tools of her long lost trade back to the gelding. As she put the saddle on the gelding he stood like a perfect gentleman. Her mom and Mally had done a good job continuing his training. Enid hadn't sat on him since he was three. At that time they were winning every 3-foot Hunter class they entered. Enid took the bridle and fitted it to the gelding's large head. He took the bit willingly, almost eagerly. She walked him out of the barn toward the indoor riding arena gathering her hat and gloves on the way.

She led him into the middle of the ring to the mounting block. She put her left foot into the stirrup. Homebody stood like a statue. Enid settled into the saddle. She had forgotten how comfortable it was. She put her right foot in the stirrup and gathered her reins slightly. As she asked Homebody to walk out, the length of his stride took her aback.

For the next 30 minutes it was like Enid was transported back in time. She knew instinctively what to do. She warmed the gelding up in walk, gathered her reins a bit more and then posted the long smooth trot, guiding the gelding in large circles and turns. She walked again with more contact, asking the gelding to compress his stride and to yield off

Going Home

her legs, stepping under himself. Trotting again on a shorter stride, Enid asked the gelding to canter. The thrusting power of the haunches nearly unseated her. Homebody was no homebody. He was a workhorse. Enid adjusted to his 3 beat stride and felt exhilaration mount in her soul. She slowed the gelding to a walk and gave him all the reins. He stretched and blew in contentment and pride.

There was a grid set up in the arena of three jumps. Enid looked down at Homebody. They were only 2'6" in height. Enid picked up the slack reins and asked Homebody to canter. He willingly agreed and Enid settled into the rhythm of his huge stride. She pointed him at the jumps and steadied herself into the half-seat position. His ears pricked forward and he gathered himself about 3 strides from the first jump. Neatly and efficiently he folded his legs and vaulted effortlessly over the obstacles. As Enid asked the gelding to trot, she felt an unfamiliar strain on her face. She was shocked to discover it was a smile that started in her heart and overflowed onto her face, ear-to-ear. As she was trotting around in her own world of contentment, a voice catapulted her back to the here and now.

"Enid, hi." It was Leonora. "You look like the cat that swallowed the canary. What's the big secret?"

"There's no secret, Leonora. It's just that I had a great ride." She paused, "It's been a long time."

"That's great, Enid" Leonora said. "Would you have time this week for another lesson?"

"Sure, how about Wednesday afternoon about 3:00 p.m? And then, if you have time, you can stay for tea. Mom will be home."

"I look forward to it." Leonora headed out to get Joe.

Enid dismounted, loosened the girth and ran the stirrups

up the saddle so that they were out of the way. She walked the gelding back to his stall, untacked him and gave him a complete grooming, getting more of the loose hair off of him and onto her clothes and the stall floor. She went to the feed room and found the carrot bag. Picking out the largest carrot in the bag, she returned to Homebody and treated him to the succulent morsel.

"Big guy, I have to confess that our time together has been the best thing I've done in three years. Thanks."

Homebody rested his head on Enid's chest. She scratched behind his ears thoughtfully, feeling the empty chamber in her soul begin to fill up.

Chapter Twelve

The visit with her mom that night was the first time in a long while that Enid was able to steadily look her mom in the eyes. What she saw was an attractive woman in her early 50s, resonating peace and wholeness. What Enid didn't know was what she was revealing—a 23-year-old back on the road to life.

Meredith was careful not to pry too far but she knew that something had happened. She saw in Enid's face a relaxation that had been absent for so long. As casually as she could, she asked Enid about her day. A glow started to radiate from Enid's eyes and it affected every aspect of her being.

"I rode Homebody today," Enid said trying to sound unimpressed.

Meredith showed no reaction. "Oh, and how was he?"

Enid looked at her mom trying unsuccessfully to match her unassuming speech. "Mom, you know how he is. He's awesome!"

Meredith looked up from her hands into her daughter's

shining face. It took every ounce of resolve not to burst into tears. Instead she turned the energy into laughter. "He is something, isn't he?"

Enid joined in the revelry. "I should say. I only jumped the grid of 3 fences and they are only set at 2'6" but that revealed quite a bit." Enid settled to ask professionally, "What are your plans for the boy?"

Meredith became serious. "I plan on finding someone to bring him and the others along this year, then sell them for as much as I can get. Hopefully, they're my ticket out of the arena loan."

Meredith searched Enid's face. Enid inhaled deeply. She had feared as much. As wonderful as Homebody was, if he was her mom's ticket to some breathing room, Enid would do all she could without getting in the way or complicating things.

"I'll ride him and get him as fit and as ready as I can for you while I'm here," she smiled comfortingly, "and that goes for all the Young Guns."

Meredith could not hold the second wave of emotion back. She let the tears pour, come what may. "E, you have no idea how much that means to me to hear you say that."

Enid reached for her mom and embraced her. "I think I might have a bit of an idea." Meredith smiled through the stream of tears. "Thank you E, you've made my day."

"Does that mean Dr. Brown hasn't been here yet?" Enid asked teasingly.

"What do you mean by that remark?" Meredith asked coyly.

"You two seem, what shall I say, comfortable with one another." Enid was grinning from ear to ear, giving her face muscles another work out.

Going Home

"I'm sure I don't know what you're talking about," Meredith sighed. "We're just old friends."

"Well, I'll agree with the old part," Enid chuckled, "But I suspect the friend part might have evolved into something more." Enid glanced at her mom. "I don't mind, you know, in fact I quite approve if that holds any weight at all."

"You know it does, E. Ted and I would never consider changing things if it upset our children," she looked up at Enid, "you and Mally always wanted to be sisters."

Meredith paused searching Enid's face. "You should go in and see her while you're here," she said softly.

"I don't know, Mom, what would I say?"

"You don't have to say anything. Remember how Mally was there for you?"

Enid felt a jolt go through her. "There for me? I remember her going on with the wedding when I begged her not to." Enid's voice rose from light-hearted banter to cutting sarcasm in a millisecond.

"E, you're not remembering correctly. The funeral was in late April and the wedding in the middle of July. There was no reason for Mally to postpone her wedding. Your dad certainly would not have wanted her to." Meredith took a long slow breath praying for the right words.

"E, let go of that and think back to the day after your dad and Home Boy died." Meredith breathed again. "Mally was there. She never left you."

Enid unwillingly let herself be transported back to the pain-filled days. She couldn't remember much. Dr. Nichol had had to administer a narcotic for the first three days as Enid was so overcome with grief she was incoherent. What she did remember were two voices, two sets of hands: Mom's and Mally's. She had been there for her, fed her, dressed her, and even got her to the bathroom and shower. Mally had taken over all of Enid's chores in the barn. Took over the teaching and training during the busiest time in her life, the last few months before her wedding. Enid's face was washed in a salty flow again. She wouldn't have made it through those days if it weren't for Mally. Homestead Farms wouldn't have made it through the last three years without Mally. How did Enid repay her? She let her do everything in the barn, was no better than a apparition at her wedding, and then ran away to Vancouver the first chance she got without even so much as a thank you or a goodbye.

"I've been such an idiot, Mom," Enid cried.

"Just go to her honey. It will be alright, I promise."

Enid wiped off her face. "How can I go to her now?"

"The best way would be to walk into her room and give her a hug," Meredith said softly.

Enid straightened up. Her mom was always direct and practical. This outlook had served her well as a wife, mother, riding instructor and horse trainer. She needed to be more like her mom, she needed to grow up.

"What room is she in?"

"Second floor, room 6A" was all her mom said.

Enid found the room quicker than she was ready for. Peeking in, she saw Mally lying on the hospital bed looking as pale and fragile as the Lady of Shallot on her barge. Enid lightly knocked, hoping that Mally wouldn't awaken and then she would be released from her obligation. No such luck. Mally turned her pretty face to the door. Her dull eyes lightened at Enid's appearance.

"E, is that you?" she asked weakly.

"Yes," Enid approached the bed.

"How's your mom?"

Going Home

Classic Mally, still thinking of everyone but herself.

"She's feeling better and can't wait to get out of here tomorrow."

"Me too," Mally added quietly.

Enid sat on her bed and timidly reached out her hand. Mally grabbed it and squeezed it lightly. Enid squeezed back. Mally gave it three quick squeezes, Enid responded with three longer ones and Mally finished it off with three more quick squeezes. An old childhood code.

"SOS," Mally said tearfully.

Enid reached over, enveloping Mally's slight frame in her arms. They hugged and cried together, letting the years wash away between them.

Mally spoke first, "E, I've missed you so much."

Enid sobbed louder, "I've been such an idiot. I'm so sorry for everything."

"There's nothing to be sorry for, E." Mally said firmly.

"I've been so selfish, so unfeeling for so long. I've cut off everyone I love from my life. I haven't really been alive for a long time." Mally hugged her harder. Enid continued, "I'm so sorry you lost your baby. Oh Mally, I'm so sorry."

It was Mally's turn to sob into Enid's arms. When the waves of grief subsided, the girls parted and looked at each other. Mally's pale face had a bit of color spring onto her cheeks. The death pallor that had shadowed Enid's face was losing its dominance. They each managed a smile. They were holding hands. Enid used Morse code for "I love you." Mally returned it. They laughed and hugged each other.

"How long can you stay and help your mom?" Mally finally spoke.

"I have a six week leave of absence. I think I'll be using it all." She looked hard at Mally. "Mom's selling Homestead

87

Farms. She's lost her passion for it and wants to travel and see the world. I need to stay and help her get the horses fit and going so she can get a good price for them."

"When I gain some strength back I'll help you," Mally offered.

"Really? That would be great. I could really use the help. I'll figure some way to pay you. I promise."

"It's not about the money, E. I don't want to be a burden. I want to be a help," Mally stated.

"I know, however, we will work something out," Enid put on her negotiation demeanor, "and just what do you know of the budding romance between our parents?"

Mally managed a broad smile. "No facts, but my overactive imagination has been working overtime. Is there really something there besides an old friendship?" Mally queried.

"I think that spring is in the air in more than one sense."

Tim walked into the room at that moment. The sight he saw made the sorrow flee away from him. His joy was renewed as he looked at his wife shining with happiness. "Can I join the circle?" he asked shyly.

Enid looked at Tim with a mixture of pain and joy. She let go of one of Mally's hands. "I think it's time to reunite the Three Musketeers."

Chapter Thirteen

Enid came home from her meeting with Midwell and Stephans in a sober mood. Her mom had a healthy net worth. The problem was that all her money was tied up and not easily liquidated. Her father's pension didn't kick in until Meredith was fifty-five. That was in three years. The arena loan would be paid off the same year. $60,000 was left on the principle and though there was no mortgage on the property, Meredith didn't want to borrow against it. Enid didn't blame her. The monthly expenses had slowly and surely exceeded the monthly income as Meredith boarded fewer horses and taught fewer lessons. What Homestead Farms needed was an influx of good old hard cash. Enid could see that if her mom sold the Young Guns she would be free and clear. The ponies weren't a problem, as her mom could easily find homes for them all. And Homecoming Queen, her mom's baby, was going nowhere. Enid sighed. It would be difficult on everyone in the family to sell Homestead Farms. Although Mike and Elizabeth lived in Kelowna, they enjoyed coming back to the island. Mike had all of his school buddies here to go fishing with and Elizabeth enjoyed the safe environment for her twins, Donny and Dina. Lucy would be the least affected as she had already sold most of her stuff and was bent on staying in Africa. When Mom sold the property she would have no financial worries for the rest of her life and would be free to follow her heart wherever that led.

Tuesday's Pony Club lessons went better than Enid had expected. The E's all came at once in a cacophony of childish squeals, pony whinnies, and parental voices. Hannah Wilson, 6, rode the pony she shared with her older brothers Harry, 8, a D and Kyle, 10, a D2. Digger was a respectable 14 hh black pony of unknown origin. He was sturdy and docile, the perfect family pet. Joanna Babcock also rode the family horse. Charlie was a gray quarter horse cross and was a very round 14.2 hh. David Babcock and the Wilson boys went off to play in the field. The other E members rode Homestead Farms ponies. Meghan Graham, 6, on Davy Crocket, Roberta Grey, 7, on Jesse James, and Jordan Atwell, 8, on Annie Oakley. All the moms were friendly and helpful. Enid could see that the club was healthy despite the lack of C members.

Ede and Ada had come out early to help Enid get the ponies ready. They had noticed a difference in Mr. Big as soon as they had entered the barn. Enid had given the Larkes ladies the lowdown on Mr. Big. He had to respect them and if he showed any dominant behavior he was to be tied up and left for 15 minutes. Enid also showed them how to use lunging as a training time. She had Ada put Mr. Big through the paces of walk, trot, canter and halt on cue. When he was lazy then Enid encouraged Ada to get bigger

Going Home

by standing on her toes and swishing the lunge whip toward the pony. Enid showed her how to give the commands like she meant business. If there was no reaction, she was to snap the lunge whip. Mr. Big was a smart pony and once Ada had the skills, he knew he was beat. He tried the next trick. Take off running pell-mell at the end of the line. Enid showed Ada how to hold the line in a safe and secure manner and how to use her body language to slow the pony down.

"If you position yourself more to his shoulder and neck he'll slow down. If you're more to his hind end he'll speed up and if you're across from his withers he should maintain his pace."

Ada and Ede both took turns experimenting with their body position and Ede was very encouraged. Enid's time with Mr. Big was good that day too. His attitude in the stall had improved 150%. Earlier that day, Enid had saddled him, bridled him and rode him around the arena popping him over the fences for about an hour. He was clever and athletic, a top-notch pony. Whatever had been bothering the fetlock last week was cleared up. He seemed to be willing enough for Enid. The real test would come when Ada got on him in the arena with all the other D's.

As Enid put the E's through their paces, memories came flooding back. Not only of when she was in pony club trotting around this very ring with her club mates, but also of teaching the Pony Club before she left. It saddened her that not one of them was still involved.

Enid let the E's finish their lesson by doing an around-the-world exercise. It was the old favorite of pony clubbers around the world. Every young rider was scared at first to sit sidesaddle then maneuver until they were facing backwards. That always brought the giggles on before the riders continued around to sit sidesaddle once more before finishing off so that they were back where they started from: facing the pony's ears. Enid dismissed them and got ready for the D's. The moms helped Enid get the E's off the ponies and the D's on.

Melanie Graham, 8, rode Annie Oakley. Harry Wilson took Digger's reins from Hannah. Anne Marie Landsbury, 9, came out leading Wild Bill Hickock. Last, but certainly not least, Ada appeared on Mr. Big. After they all mounted up, Enid had them walk head to tail in a single file around the arena. She led them in a few exercises at the walk and then moved them into a trot. Enid watched the students with a critical eye. She could tell that her mom had used her methodical and safe instruction practices on the students. She really didn't expect anything less. All the kids had a safe basic position. After a few figures of eight and serpentines, an ess pattern ridden back and forth across the arena, she called them into the center of the ring.

"Does anyone have any questions?" Enid asked.

"When do we get to jump?" Ada ventured out feeling more comfortable around Enid than the rest of the group.

"How much have you done?" returned Enid.

"We've done poles and cross poles," Melanie said.

"And Mrs. Taylor let us do a 2' Hunter course at the play day," Anne Marie added.

"Please, Miss Taylor?" Ada chirped in.

"Harry, how do you feel about it?" Enid asked the lone boy.

"It's fun," was all he said.

"Okay, then, next week we'll do some jumping but right now I need to see your canter work."

By the time Enid was back in the house she was

Going Home

exhausted. Honest exhaustion, earned exhaustion. She made herself a hot cheese omelet and whole-wheat toast with strawberry jam. Not even the best sushi in Vancouver compared to this simple meal. As she reflected on the events of the day she couldn't help but wonder how she was going to fit back into the city life.

Chapter Fourteen

Enid was in the barn early on Wednesday morning. She wanted everything to be ready for when the vet arrived. Dr. Brown was right on time.

"Good morning, Enid. How's it going?" Jacob inquired sincerely.

"Good, although I will confess to you that I'm finding it rather hard to walk today," Enid confided.

"Ah, the third day. You must have been riding?" He formed it as a question.

"You could say that." Enid said.

She had already lunged Homemaker and was pleased with her attitude to work. She was gangly, as three-year-olds were prone to be, yet her stride showed the promise of length and lightness which her mom was so famous for passing on. There was no resistance to the saddle or bridle and Enid was counting the days before she would be sitting on her back.

Home Hunter had jumped the 3' course Enid set out like a pro and she was beginning to plan his spring show calendar.

He was aptly named, as he possessed the premium canter stride looked for in first class hunters: efficient, rhythmic and balanced. Enid had already listed him on the Internet, hoping for a California connection to get top dollar.

She had given Homebody a bit more of a challenge today. She had looked up his last years show records and saw that Mally had taken him in the local 3'3" Hunters and Jumpers. He had done well enough in the Hunters to gain the year-end Reserve Championship even though he had only made it to a few shows. In the Jumpers he had placed in every class.

Mally was a good rider and very compassionate towards the horse. She had a classic Hunt Seat position and was difficult to beat in Equitation classes where the rider's position and effectiveness is judged, however she was too laid back for the jumpers. She just didn't possess the killer instinct required for the tight, near impossible turns and the speed necessary to win against the clock.

Enid had set up a jumping lane of 4 jumps ascending in height from 3' to 4'6." After warming the gelding up on the flat, concentrating on suppling exercises, Enid had put him through the chute. He ate up the jumps. Enid could feel him snap his knees up with conviction every time. 4'6" was barely a challenge for this boy. Enid reveled in the exhilaration of being thrust past gravity and, for a moment in time, being suspended in the air connected with a partner so wild and powerful, yet yielded to her guidance. She only put the gelding through the chute twice because of his lack of fitness but the small taste was enough to awaken in her something buried deep in her core. *This is what I was born to do*, she thought. At that moment Enid had felt more alive than at any moment since receiving the A rating for pony club. Just

Going Home

the thought of riding the gelding again brought the swell of purpose back to the forefront.

"Let me introduce you to the gang."

She led Jacob into the barn where the ponies were all poking their heads out of the stall windows curiously. Enid had locked them in so they had no access to their runs. They were not impressed. "We have Davy Crockett, Wild Bill Hickock, Doc Holiday, Jesse James and Annie Oakley." Enid waited for the response to come.

"You weren't kidding when you said 'gang' were you?" Jacob laughed warmly.

He started with Davy Crockett and worked his way through the ponies. They each had their teeth filed smooth from any sharp edges, received their yearly shots and had a general check up. There were no surprises; the ponies had always been well looked after.

"Do you have time for a coffee?" Enid asked.

"No, but I do have time for lunch. You didn't forget did you?" Jacob smiled at her.

"No, I mean, yes, I did forget," Enid looked sheepishly at Jacob. "Sorry, I guess I've been rather distracted. There's been so much to think about and do. I don't know how my mom did it all these years plus be a wife and mother! I have a whole new respect for her."

"Yeah, I understand what you're saying. The hours my uncle keeps are insane. How did he do it when he had small children? And he coached soccer every year that Mally played but I guess you know that since you were on the same team."

"Yeah, Dr. Brown is a great guy. I'm glad my mom and him are exploring new depths of their friendship," Enid sneaked a peek at Jacob's face.

"You knew didn't you?" she asked accusingly.

"Yes, but you have to understand Uncle Ted just needed another guy to talk to. Someone not involved. I rolled into town and he unloaded on me," Jacob grinned. "It was kind of cool actually, he sounded like a teenager in love for the first time."

As they were laughing, Dr. Brown's truck rolled up the driveway. Enid reached the passenger door before it came to a stop.

"Mom, welcome home," Enid opened the door.

Meredith looked tired but happy. Her leg was supported in an air cast and there was a new pair of crutches on the seat in the back.

"E, dear. Thank you. But I thought you and Jacob would be out for lunch by now. You didn't cancel it for me did you?"

"No Mom, we were just leaving but are you going to be okay? We don't have to go today. I don't want to leave you alone as soon as you get home."

"I picked up lunch for us," said Dr. Brown. He held up a take out bag from Chan's Kitchen.

"Oh, I see," Enid grinned, "and since you both know Chinese is not my favorite I take the hint. Jacob, shall we go?"

Jacob laughed, "Well, there go my plans for a nice Chinese lunch."

"Oh, no, you're not serious?" Enid groaned.

"No, I'm just teasing. I was thinking more along the lines of the Old House."

"Jacob, I believe you're operating on inside information."

"I confess. I did use the resources around me to pry

Going Home

out pertinent information on the enigma known as Enid Taylor."

"He asked me," confessed Ted Brown. "I hope you don't mind that I revealed your culinary preferences." There was a definitive tongue in cheek tone to Dr. Brown's confession.

"Not at all. I love The Old House Restaurant. Have you been yet, Jacob?" Before he could answer Enid continued, "Not only is the food divine but the atmosphere is world class."

"With an endorsement like that let's go. I'm starving."

Over lunch Jacob and Enid talked of life in the Comox Valley as compared to Vancouver and Guelph, Ontario. Enid had been to Toronto once. Her parents had surprised the family with a trip to Toronto to attend the Royal Winter Fair. Enid saw the world's top show jumpers in action indoors. It was breath taking to see them gallop and turn in such a tight space—a very different game than outdoors where the Grand Prix Field was gigantic in proportion. It had been in November, not the best time to judge southern Ontario for livability. Jacob had grown up in rural Ontario and was finding the atmosphere in the Comox Valley similar.

"I'm sure you'll notice a difference in the weather though," Enid advised.

"I'm definitely looking forward to the first winter day I'm playing golf. I'll be the one phoning home and bragging the way Uncle Ted has done since I can remember."

Enid laughed. Her father and brother were both avid golfers and being true West Coast cronies did the phone call back east routine at least once a year. *No wonder people in the East think that British Columbians are all rednecks,* Enid thought.

"Thank you so much for lunch," Enid said over the coffee. "I've missed this place."

"I think your endorsement was lacking. You didn't tell me of the wonderful gardens or that it was on the riverside," Jacob noted.

"Words don't do the place justice. I always wish walls really could talk when I'm in here. There must be great stories from over the years. Weddings, parties, family Christmas mornings," Enid sighed. I'm going to really miss Homestead Farms when my mom sells it. I've known no other home."

"I thought you owned a condo in Vancouver?" Jacob inquired.

"Owning a condo and living in it doesn't really make it a home. I thought it did a week ago," Enid said wistfully.

"Yeah, I guess you're right. I lived on campus at college and never made it home. Uncle Ted has opened his house to me for as long as I want and being family it feels like home so I'm lucky," Jacob smiled, "But don't be sad quite yet. Your mom hasn't even listed it. It could be a while before you have to pack up and leave."

"That's true. There is a lot of work to be done. The buildings are all sound so there is no problem there. The house could use some updating but nothing major, like a roof, is necessary. It's the landscaping. Usually my mom's garden is thriving but it doesn't look as if she's done anything since last summer. I have a brown thumb at the very least. My sister Lucy is the nurturer. But now that mom is home she can at least supervise. I didn't dare even pull anything out of the beds before she got home."

"Well, if you need some extra help, just call. Gardening happens to be my other source of anti-stressing besides golf."

Going Home

"I may just take you up on the offer if you're not careful," Enid teased. "Mally has offered to come and help with the Young Guns after she gains some strength back," she added.

"Tim mentioned you had been up to see her," Jacob reached over and took Enid's hand. She looked into his mesmerizing eyes. "I'm glad."

Enid didn't feel any ulterior motives in the touch from Jacob. What she felt was camaraderie. This in no way disappointed her. She wasn't looking for romance and apparently neither was Jacob. They each needed a friend. They each had found one.

"Me too," Enid said quietly. "I don't know why I waited so long."

"God has the timing for everything in our lives. I don't mean that in a glib manner. I truly believe it. I came to a point in my life where I had to decide if I was going to believe God. I don't mean believe in God or what Jesus did on the cross. I mean believe that God is truly God, truly sovereign. So much garbage, cruelty and pain is in this world it's hard to understand Jesus has everything under His authority. He doesn't seem just at times."

"I know that feeling," Enid said with conviction.

"I want to share with you a bit of my journey," Jacob paused. Enid could see that he was composing himself, controlling his emotions.

"A year ago I was engaged to my high school sweetheart, Katherine. We were to be married this May. In January she went missing. She didn't show up for work one morning. She ran a daycare out of the church she attended. The police came and interviewed me. I guess the fiancé is always a good suspect even if they live in a different province. Katherine was living in Montreal. They found her three days later. She had been raped and murdered." Jacob stopped and despite his attempts at control his eyes filled. He shut them tight. Enid took his other hand and just held them. He continued.

"I've wrestled with God for the last three months but before I came here I decided to believe God. He never leaves us or forsakes us. He didn't leave Katherine. He didn't forsake her. This world is not my home. This world was not Katherine's home. His ways and thoughts are higher than mine. I can't understand His ways because I am not God," Jacob took a breath and then looked at Enid squarely.

"Every morning I wake up and ask God for the mind of Christ. I ask that He live through me. I ask for the power of the Holy Spirit to fill me because I can't live this life alone. I need Him. Jesus left the Holy Spirit here on earth for that very reason. He knows our ways. He knows our thoughts before we speak them. He is our Creator and knows us even better than we know ourselves. I can't live without my relationship with God. To cut Him out would be to slit my own throat. So I choose life everyday. It isn't easy. I've had a lot of people try to help me in their own inadequate ways. Some of what they said was really unfeeling but their hearts were right. They didn't mean to be offensive. They just didn't know what to do or say. Who does? I had to look past that and even if I didn't trust them or know them I choose to let Christ be the judge." He smiled weakly, "I don't mean to preach. Sorry."

"Don't be sorry. You didn't preach at me. You shared with me. Thank you," Enid looked away. "I've cut God out of my life. I don't know if I can make the leap back. I just don't know."

Jacob squeezed her hands. "It's okay, Enid, just know

Going Home

that Mally and Tim, Uncle Ted, your mom and I are there for you and praying for you." Jacob looked at his watch, "I guess I'd better get back to my rounds. I have a herd of swine calling my name."

Enid appreciated Jacob's sensitivity. He knew how to change gears without grinding them.

She arrived back at the farm at 2:50 p.m. Dr. Brown had left and her mom was resting upstairs in her room. When she looked at the grandfather clock in the kitchen, she remembered that she had promised Leonora a lesson. She quickly changed and then went down to the barn.

"Hi," Enid greeted Leonora and Joe, "sorry I'm late."

"No problem," came the friendly reply, "we were just working on the position changes you suggested the other day. I'm having a hard time keeping the inner thigh muscle on the saddle. I've ridden around for years the wrong way. You might be able to teach an old gal some new tricks but I'm fighting muscle memory," Leonora chuckled.

"You're doing great," Enid said encouragingly. "As you're walking around go up into the two-point position. Grab some mane to make it easier and so you don't accidentally catch Joe with the bit. Good. Stretch the heels down. Now sit and one leg at a time turn the thigh muscle in by taking your foot out of the stirrup stretch it down and back, good and place it back into your stirrup. Let's move up to posting trot."

Enid worked Leonora for a good 30 minutes and was pleased once more with the pair. She hadn't taught many adults and was finding it fun. There was less pressure. Leonora rode because she enjoyed it, period. There were no outside expectations put on her by peers, parents, or a program.

While Leonora cooled Joe out and groomed him, Enid

went up to the house to make tea. Her mom was downstairs by that time and greeted her with a smile and a wink.

"How goes the battle in the barn?" Meredith inquired.

"Great, how was your lunch? And when were you going to tell me about Dr. Brown and you?" Enid asked teasingly.

"What's to tell?" came the mysterious answer.

"You tell me," Enid shot back.

"Ted and I are old friends. Our families have known each other for over twenty years."

"Tell me something I don't know," probed Enid.

"Ted and I have been meeting for coffee the last few months. It happened by accident actually," Meredith sounded almost apologetic. "It was in February, near Valentine's Day. I was feeling sorry for myself amidst the sweetheart and 'couple' stuff. One morning after I fed the horses, I just couldn't return to an empty house. I couldn't endure another cup of coffee staring at that empty chair." She pointed at the old recliner. "So I headed for Tim Horton's. When I walked in and got in line Ted was just in front of me. I didn't see him because I didn't want to see anyone. It's weird. I couldn't stand being alone yet I didn't want to see anyone. I wanted to be alone among people," Meredith stopped.

"I understand, Mom," Enid had lived that way for the last three years.

"Well the line moved but I hadn't noticed. I was zoned out, in my own little world. The lady behind me basically pushed me and I bumped into Ted. He turned around and when I went to apologize we saw each other. Naturally we sat together. We talked about old times and about adjusting to being alone. It was safe. It was familiar. So we decided to meet the following week and so on," Meredith paused. Enid waited. Surly there was more to it than that.

Going Home

"And…" Enid gestured for more.

"And what?"

"And how did it become more than friends?"

"It's not more than friends, I mean we haven't kissed or anything. Hey, wait a minute. I'm the mom, you're the daughter. I don't have to explain anything to you. Do I?"

"You mean you aren't more than friends?" Enid asked inquiringly.

"I don't know. I mean, yes, but no. I don't know! I'm confused. What did you ask me?"

"Mom, you're being impossible," Enid laughed. "If you are not more than friends then what has changed between you and Dr. Brown?"

"I guess you could say we're exploring our options."

Before Enid could pry any further, the door opened.

"Hello?"

"Hi Leonora, you're just in time to save me from my daughter's interrogations," Meredith chimed.

"Oh, I'm sorry if I interrupted anything," Leonora said sincerely.

"No you didn't. It's good." Meredith turned to her daughter, "E, Leonora likes the ginger tea. I think I'll have some too." She winked at her friend, "It's great having a maid. I always wanted one." The two women chuckled.

"Very funny," Enid retorted as she poured the steaming water into the mugs. The pungent smell filled the kitchen. While the older women talked, Enid put on her mother's fanciest apron and put the tea on a tray accompanied by a plate of cookies. She carried it in and said in her best English accent. "M'lady, tea is served."

Meredith and Leonora looked up and the three of them burst into giggles.

Chapter Fifteen

Thursday morning Enid awoke to the smell of fresh coffee and pancakes. She looked at her clock, thinking that she had slept through her alarm. It was 6:45 a.m. She had been getting out of bed at 7:00 to feed by 7:30. Her mom had always been an early riser but Enid assumed a broken leg would have slowed her down a bit. She should have known better.

Enid appeared in the kitchen 10 minutes later in her jeans and old high school sweater. Her mom was sitting in front of a small fire reading her Bible. She looked up as Enid walked in.

"Good morning sweetie. Coffee's on," Meredith looked content and comfortable.

"Yes, I know. The overpowering aroma woke me up," Enid kidded. "I thought I was supposed to take care of you and you were going to join the royal ranks with Queenie."

"I couldn't help myself. As nice as St. Joseph is, for a

hospital, you just can't survive on the food. I got out just in time."

Enid laughed. She knew her mom loved being in the kitchen. She always told Enid that instead of eating under stress, she baked. Enid and her siblings secretly stressed her out on purpose just so she would bake her famous Monster Cookies.

"I suppose I can eat before the horses for once," Enid went to the oven and loaded up two plates with pancakes and bacon. She added sliced oranges and poured maple syrup over the top.

"Do you want your breakfast there or are you hobbling over to the table?"

"I'm hobbling," Meredith replied. She put her Bible down and picked up her crutches. She managed to limp her way to the table. Enid retrieved her cup and poured them both fresh coffees.

"So, what are your plans today?" Meredith asked.

"I'll work the Young Guns this morning and then I'll plan the Pony Club lessons for the afternoon."

"Sounds good. I think I'll come out when you're riding," her mom said firmly.

"I don't think you're suppose to be up and about for too long. Aren't you supposed to keep your leg elevated as much as possible?" Enid asked, trying not to sound bossy.

"I'm not doing anything too spectacular today. The boys jumped yesterday so I was going to go out and do some intervals to build up their fitness. Homemaker is still being lunged. I'll wait to ride her so that you can be out there, next week," Enid gave her mom the look that Meredith had used to perfection in raising her kids. One look from Mom and everything stopped.

Going Home

Meredith backed down. "Okay, I suppose I shouldn't risk ending up back in the hospital quite yet. I'm just tired of sitting around."

"Why don't you go online and download some show programs and start planning the spring schedule. Home Hunter can do the 3' Hunters. I don't think he should do jumpers. We'll get more money for him if we keep him concentrating on one thing at this point. Did I tell you that I advertised him on the Internet?" Enid asked her mom.

"No, you didn't mention it. Is that a good thing? How could we be sure he would get a good home?"

"Mom, just because you advertise doesn't mean you have to take the first offer that comes along. I hope you don't mind, though, I've kind of taken over their training. Are you okay with that?"

"E, they've sat around for the last six weeks. I'm more than okay with the fact that you've picked up where Mally and I left off. I'm thrilled."

"I'm glad. I'm looking forward to riding Homemaker. She's so gawky right now but the potential is there for all to see, at least anyone that has an eye for horses. Once I back her, we'll see if she'll go to any shows this year. Homebody, on the other hand, we'll start in the 3'6" Jumpers, but I'd like to get him to the 4' division as soon as possible. He's more than able. He lacks fitness and a balanced galloping stride but that will come. If I remember correctly he fits up quite fast like Home Boy."

"Yes, he does. They're full brothers, remember," Meredith reminded her.

"It's hard to forget. He's so similar sometimes I think it is Home Boy," Enid grew quiet.

"You know, Enid, if Home Boy could, he would apply

the spurs you used on him as encouragement to go forward. Remember the water jump at Michael Lake? You never wanted to wear spurs but Home Boy was having none of that water jump. You had to put them on and apply them to further his training and to show him that you were trustworthy and you wouldn't ask him to do anything beyond what he was able. God promises us the same thing in 1 Corinthians. He's trustworthy. So be spurred on. Homebody needs you to ride him. Mally is awesome but we all know that you're the jumper rider in the group."

"Well, I certainly was never the equitation rider, despite having the best instructor around. Mally beat me every time!" Enid said lightly.

"And you beat her every time in the jump-off. Though I do remember Tim having some success over you."

"Tim was an excellent rider. It's too bad he quit after his C2. He could have made it all the way with the right horse."

"Well, he loved to play football and that took over in high school. It's hard being a male English rider in high school. Not too bad if you ride bulls in this town, but jumpers? Tim did well riding through junior high school."

"That's true enough," Enid looked at her watch, "I better go and feed the beasties."

The day went smoothly. Ede and Ada helped Enid get ready for the pony club lessons. Enid was finding Ede to be a knowledgeable and capable District Commissioner for the Merville Pony Club.

The D1's, Susan and Shannon McDonald, were 10-year-old twins. They rode Jesse James and Annie Oakley. Their position was solid and Enid was pleased to see that they were both keen to improve and move up a level. Enid

GOING HOME

set up a gymnastic grid of trot poles leading to a cross bar jump and then one stride to a small vertical, or upright fence. The ponies were on autopilot through the grid so Susan and Shannon could concentrate on their positions. Enid encouraged them to drop the reins once past the trotting poles and put their arms out like wings. The twins loved it and after about the 5th time through Enid saw the desired result, a quieter upper body and a steadier leg.

The D2's arrived in good time for their lesson. Everyone seemed eager to ride. The air was energized with the curiosity a substitute teacher conjures up.

Kyle Wilson rode the family pony, Digger. David Babcock was astride the family horse, Charlie. Enid had seen these ponies the other day and was pleased with their temperaments and abilities. Ruth Genung, a tall 11-year-old, came out on Wild Bill. In spite of his name, the thoroughbred cross gelding was quite docile and laid back. Hillary Daniels and Amelia Ormand arrived together in a brand new aluminum 2-horse gooseneck trailer. There were living quarters in the front area. Enid was quite impressed. The girls led their horses down the ramp. Both horses were chestnuts. Both looked like they belonged in the pricey trailer. Hillary's mare had four high socks and a wide blaze. She had a delicate dished face. Amelia's mount was a gelding, sporting a rich caramel coat highlighted by a flaxen mane and tail. He didn't have a white hair on him. Both horses were about 16.hh and gleamed in the afternoon sun. They had their saddles on and it took the girls only a moment to bridle up and join the other D2's in the arena.

Enid told the students to warm the horses up on their own. She watched them walk and trot around the arena with an educated eye. The boys moved quickly through the paces.

They wasted little time walking. They were soon trotting and cantering around the arena. Every once in a while they did a circle.

Ruth did precisely five minutes of walk, making sure she went both directions. She proceeded at trot and rode a pattern down the long wall, 20-meter circle, across the diagonal and then she repeated it. This lasted for another five minutes. She then cantered and repeated the trot pattern with a simple change of lead at the imaginary letter X in the center of the arena. Enid smiled inwardly, recognizing her mother's influence on the young girl.

Hillary and Amelia rode around without a clear plan. They rode side by side talking to one another. Amelia mimicked whatever Hillary did. When she finally did go off on her own she cantered in the opposite direction of everyone else. She didn't follow the arena rule, which states that riders should pass left hand to left hand. At one point she nearly collided with Hillary. Neither girl was looking up or paying attention.

Enid called them into the center of the arena and talked about the goals of a warm up. Not one of the students had done any lateral work: leg-yield, turn on the haunches, or a turn on the forehand. These exercises sharpened the horse to the rider's leg aids. Enid started the lesson by having the students practice each movement. Although the D2's had learned each of these movements, they didn't fully appreciate the application of them. After the horses each performed the exercises to Enid's approval, she let the D2's jump the grid she had set up for the D1's. Hillary complained that the jumps were too small. She informed Enid that she was going to move up to the 3' level of Hunters and Jumpers this year and didn't want to jump anything smaller. Amelia, on the other

Going Home

hand found the exercise just right. The boys also thought the jumps were too small and Ruth didn't care one way or the other. Enid explained that this was the warm up only and that she would raise the jumps to the D2 level of 2'6" if the horses and riders were going through competently.

Kyle was the first to negotiate his way through the line of jumps. He did just fine. Digger was a cute jumper. He snapped his knees up as if he was being asked to jump around an Olympic Show Jumping course. David was next to jump through the grid. His position needed some work. He tended to tip his shoulder forward at the jump. This was always a good excuse for a pony to put on the breaks but Charlie was as honest as the day is long and packed him through the grid time and again. Enid watched as Ruth approached the jumps. She knew Wild Bill. He was an honest safe jumper. Ruth sailed through the grid in a secure and effective position. Hillary approached the series of jumps. She and her mare, Lilac Lass, looked professional and polished through the grid. Enid had to admit that they looked ready to do the 3' Division this spring.

Enid had found out that Hillary and Amelia boarded their horses at Tina Crooms.' She had a place near the fairgrounds and was a long established Hunter Jumper instructor. Enid knew the family well as Bekah Crooms had progressed through the Merville Pony Club to the B level alongside Enid. Bekah had quit after attaining the B level to concentrate solely on the Jumpers. With both of their moms as instructors, Bekah and Enid had a lot in common. This made them easy friends and fierce competitors.

As Enid watched Amelia pick her way over the fences she noticed that although she boarded and trained at the same facility as Hillary, she could not have been more different as a rider. While Hillary was confident and accomplished, Amelia was timid. She merely maintained a pretty Hunter position that was ineffective with her horse. Flamenco Dancer was lazy and didn't put any effort into jumping. Looking at his confirmation he should have been able to present a picture perfect bascule, yet he jumped flat and knocked the cross pole over each time through.

Enid suggested ways each rider could adjust their position and explained how it would improve their horse's performance. She then raised the cross pole to a 2'3" vertical and made the small vertical into a 2'6" oxer, or spread fence.

Kyle took Enid's advice. He concentrated on sitting quieter and made it through the higher fences smiling from ear to ear. David put into effect Enid's suggestions and was successful in not tipping his shoulder. Charlie packed him through the heightened gymnastic with no problem. David's attitude and aggression reminded Enid of a young Tim Lewes.

Ruth and Wild Bill trotted purposefully toward the jumps and executed the new height without a hitch. Hillary followed and gave Enid a superior look before she trotted away and completed the exercise in style. Then it was Amelia's turn.

Amelia started to trot and then stopped. Enid asked her to continue but she said she didn't feel ready to do the exercise. Enid tried to convince her that she was more than capable and she encouraged her to relax and move in rhythm with her horse more. Amelia wouldn't budge. Enid was dressed in breeches and boots and asked Amelia if she could take Dancer through. Amelia looked relieved and gladly dismounted.

Enid adjusted the stirrups and jumped on. Immediately

Going Home

Dancer knew something was different. Gone was the lazy docile horse. He pricked his ears, arched his neck and began to prance around like a stallion during mating season. Enid felt the raw power beneath her and wondered how such a horse landed with a little timid girl like Amelia.

Enid cantered him around once then broke to trot. She pointed the gelding to the grid and let him have his head. He trotted rhythmically through the poles and then rocked back on his round haunches and catapulted over the little vertical like it was 4' high, he took one compressed stride and then lifted off for a second time over the oxer. He cleared it by 2.' He was so proud of himself that he bucked on the landing. Enid was just about unseated. She landed on his neck and hung on for dear life. Everyone sucked in breath and waited. She regained her position then returned to the group.

"I guess I better do that again," she said with a light laugh.

All the D2's nervously joined in the laughter. All, except Amelia. Her face was as white as marble and she looked as if she was going to burst into tears.

Enid tried to reassure her, "Amelia, you have an incredible jumping horse here. He is so smart too. He figured out right away that I thought the jumps were too small so he decided to jump them bigger. I never would have guessed that he would do that so he took me by surprise. And when you ride him, he knows that you like to go slower and steadier so that's how he goes. That's called 'kid sense' and it makes a horse priceless."

"It does?" Amelia asked quietly.

"It sure does. Here I'll do an experiment. This time through the jumps I'm going to sit quietly and concentrate on letting all of my weight sink into my heels. That will make my position stronger. Then I'm going to concentrate on the jumps and reassure Dancer that they are just right. I want to jump them. Let's see if he will jump it quieter, okay?"

"Okay," Amelia said waveringly.

Enid trotted the horse in a nice big circle before turning him to the grid. When she and Dancer were headed straight for the trotting poles, Enid rose to her jumping position and waited. She talked to the gelding through the reins. She told him what she wanted. She reassured him that he was a good boy and to be steady. He went through the grid like an old campaigner, neatly tucking his legs and skimming over the surface of the rails.

As Enid walked Dancer back to the group on a loose rein, Amelia's face was beaming proudly. The other students looked at Enid with new-found respect. Even Hillary seemed impressed with the change Enid had coaxed out of the gelding.

"See, Amelia? 'Kid-sense.' If you ever decide to sell him talk to me," Enid added this, not because she was in the market for a horse, but to make Amelia question her resolve about owning and riding such an animal.

"Oh no, I could never sell Dancer," she said proudly.

"Are you ready to try the exercise now?" Enid asked.

"Yes" she answered confidently.

Enid and Amelia switched places. Enid gave her some last minute instructions reminding Amelia to secure her leg by dropping her weight into her heels. Amelia guided Dancer quietly over the grid. Dancer seemed to know just what to do. He jumped so softly that Amelia's leg barely moved. Her smile exuded confidence. Everyone could see the change. Enid finished the lesson off by having the students cool the horses down. They walked quietly around the arena on a

Going Home

loose rein for the last five minutes. The D2's each thanked Enid for the lesson as they left the arena.

Two ladies approached Enid as the kids were leaving the arena. She assumed they were Hillary and Amelia's moms.

"Hi, Miss Taylor. I'm Vivien Daniels," she extended her manicured hand. Enid shook it warmly.

"It's nice to meet you," she said.

"And I'm Cynthia Ormand," said the other well-groomed woman.

"And it's nice to meet you," Enid replied shaking her hand.

"Thank you so much for coming to our club's rescue," Vivien said warmly.

Enid was glad that the women were friendly and open. She had dreaded, when she saw the obvious wealth, that they would be standoffish. This wasn't the case at all. "I'm not really rescuing anything. I'm just taking charge till my mom and I can sort something else out."

"Thank you for getting on Dancer. I've never seen him jump like that before." Cynthia noted. "I must admit it scared me. I didn't know if I wanted Amelia to get back on him. When we bought him last year they mentioned free jumping him to 4'6" but that really didn't mean much to us. He was quiet and safe and Amelia loved him at first sight."

"How old is he?" asked Enid.

"Eight."

"That's a good age. And what about the lovely Lilac, how old is she?"

Vivien smiled, "She is lovely, isn't she? Lilac is seven this year."

"I would say that Hillary and Amelia are both lucky girls. Will I see you on Saturday for Stable Management?"

"Both the girls will be there, however Hillary can't make the Quiz Rally," Vivien answered.

"Yes, Ede told me. I'd better get back to the barn and finish up the evening chores. I'll see you on Saturday, then."

Chapter Sixteen

It wasn't until lunch on Friday that Enid realized she had been home one week. Vancouver and her job seemed like a lifetime away. She looked at her hands. There was dirt under her fingernails, the polish chipped and cracked. Her hair hadn't seen a blow-drier or a stylist since the hurried job on Sunday morning. Her make-up bag remained zippered up. Enid smiled to herself, *Ah, the simple life.*

"What are you smirking about?" her mom asked.

"How far I've come in a week. Just look at my nails!" Enid held out her hands for inspection. "What would the girls at the office say if they saw me now?"

Meredith laughed, "Hmm, I'm sure I don't know. I must say that I haven't seen you look so beautiful in a long time."

Enid blushed in spite of herself. The warmth wasn't isolated to her face. It went clear through her. So many tears over the last week, she shouldn't be surprised to feel washed, cleaned, and lighter.

"Beauty is in the eye of the beholder, Mom," Enid replied. "But I do feel at home for the first time in a long time," Enid felt a rush of emotion. She knew she was safe with her mom. She could say whatever, however, without fear of judgment or rejection yet it was still hard to open up and be honest.

"It was really hard to open my tack trunk. I had a meltdown. I don't know if it's quite finished. I didn't exactly pray to God. I yelled and screamed at him though."

"E, most people yell at God at some point in their lives. The Psalms are full of raw, messy, angry emotions. People railing at God over the injustice that surrounded them. Our emotions are not our enemy. God made us with emotions and the capacity for deep feelings of love, hate, anger, jealousy, compassion, and sympathy just to name a few. He feels all those things. Jesus felt all those things but he didn't let them dictate his life or his reactions to people or circumstance. God calls himself a jealous God, he's free to state what he hates, what makes him angry and what stirs up compassion, mercy and love from his heart. You can be, and should be, honest about how you feel, especially toward God."

"That's good because I was completely honest with him. I still feel angry that he let Daddy, Daddy..." Enid broke down, "He let him die! He let them both die! Why? What have I ever done to God? What have you ever done to deserve that? I can't understand him, I can't trust him. I don't want to!"

Enid's sobs overcame the ability of speech. She sat at the table and buried her head. Meredith got up and hobbled over to her child and enfolded her in her arms. She joined in the tears and prayed under her breath for release for her child from the pain and confusion. When Enid's sobs were

Going Home

reduced to a rasping breathing pattern, Meredith sat back down. Enid looked at her mom.

"How can you still go to church and worship such a god?"

"Because I know he is God, Enid. We are so finite, so small in the universe. Still the Creator of everything we see and know, and don't see and don't know, sent his son to earth as a human to pay the price required for us to have a relationship with him, to make a way for us to be at home with him. It says in scripture that God holds the universe in his hand yet he emptied himself of his glory and put on flesh, became human. I can't fathom a love that would sacrifice a loved one, to sentence a child to torture and death so that others, who hate me and want nothing to do with me, would have the choice weather to come to be a part of my family or not. But I do know that God is in control. He doesn't sit in Heaven and decide to zap us or make bad things happen because he is angry or disappointed in us. No, he is love. Stuff happens because stuff happens. An accident is just that, an accident. Yes, God could intervene at any time and keep bad things from happening but you must remember, E, he is not tame."

Enid looked up. Her mom had read *The Chronicles of Narnia* to the family many times. It was one of her favorite memories from childhood. Sitting in this very room, usually in the winter after dinner, hearing different stories read out loud. Aslan, the lion in *The Chronicles of Narnia*, had seemed so real. Young Enid pictured Jesus through those eyes. She understood what her mom was saying. God is love but he is not predictable or someone to be controlled like a pet.

"I wish I could jump through a picture and go to Heaven to see that it is real. To see if Dad is there."

"E, you know it's real. You know Dad is there."

"I guess. I'm just not ready to talk to God yet," Enid sniffed.

"That's okay, honey."

"I'm nervous about tonight," Enid confided, changing the subject.

"What's there to be nervous about? Mally and Tim know you better than most people. They've never wavered in their love and concern for you. Besides, it's just dinner."

"I know," Enid smiled coyly. "But Tim is cooking."

The afternoon flew by with barn chores and gardening. Meredith had convinced Enid to bring a deck chair out of the garage so she could sit and direct the weed pulling. It didn't take long for the front bed to improve in appearance. There was something therapeutic in ripping out brown withered plants from the damp earth and thinning out the weeds to make room for the flowers to breath and grow. Enid had never liked wearing gloves. She wanted to feel the dirt and the plants in her hands. She had always been tactile that way. Only after receiving a serious rope burn did she concede to the pony club standard of wearing gloves while lunging and riding a horse.

"Good thing I didn't do anything to improve my nails this morning," Enid said, "but I better do something before I go to dinner."

"I think we've made quite a good start in this bed. Maybe tomorrow we can go and pick up some bedding plants."

"Sure, I have Stable Management in the morning so, after lunch?"

"It's a date. I can't wait to get out of the house."

"Mom, you've only been home two days and I did let you out today," Enid teased.

Going Home

"I'm not complaining, E, it's just I would like to do something constructive."

"You got the spring schedule set. That's a huge help. I have a lot of work to do the next two weeks. Quiz Rally is in one week and then the next is the first show."

"The pony clubbers should be ready," Meredith noted.

"I guess I'll find out tomorrow morning. I'd better go in and get cleaned up for dinner. Do you want me to help you, Mom?"

"No, I think I'll sit out here a while yet. Ted's coming over later with dinner. I'm going to have to cook for him sometime soon," Meredith stated.

"He's not bringing Chinese again, is he?"

"No, pizza."

"Pizza?"

"Yes, pizza and a movie."

"Well, I hope you two teenagers have fun."

"Very funny, E. Just cause we're over 50 doesn't mean we can't eat pizza or watch a movie on a Friday night."

"Just kidding, Mom," Enid said as she went in to get ready.

Dr. Brown arrived as predicted with pizza and a movie. Enid noticed her mom light up as soon as he walked in the door. She smiled warmly at them both before driving off in the Crossfire.

Although she had never been to Mally and Tim's house, she knew where it was. Tim had been living in it before the wedding. Enid pulled into the drive and wondered how Mally could live in this quiet subdivision after growing up in the country. Then again how could Enid live in a condo in False Creek and work in downtown Vancouver? With these thoughts and a thousand memories swirling around in her mind, Enid started to panic. What was she doing here? She sat frozen to her seat when a familiar Dakota truck pulled in behind her. Waves of relief washed over her. She broke free from the leather and opened the driver side door. Jacob walked up to her extending his hand in order to help her out of the low car.

"Fancy meeting you here," Jacob said conspiratorially.

"I must admit this is a pleasant surprise. I was just wondering how I was going to get through the evening being the third wheel," Enid said lightly.

"I actually invited myself," Jacob confessed. "I phoned last night to see if Mally was up for a visit and Tim mentioned you were coming for dinner. Seemed like a good time to come. Shall we?" he turned his attention to the sleek silver sports car. "What would it take to get a ride in your car?"

Enid laughed. "Would you be satisfied in the passenger seat?"

"Well, I would be content but not satisfied. I am a man after all."

Enid laughed as they made their way to the front steps. Each of the four concrete steps that led up to the pretty burgundy door was decorated with a clay pot spilling over in riotous color and heady fragrance. Enid admired the tulips, daffodils and hyacinths. Spring flowers exuded such hope. Before she could ring the bell Tim opened the door.

"Hi, come on in," Tim stepped aside to let them enter.

They joined him on the small landing. There were six steps leading up to the living room and the twin set leading down to the basement. Neutral colors decked the walls and floor giving a clean and homey atmosphere to the interior.

"Hmm, something smells good. I guess I didn't need that cheeseburger after all."

Going Home

"Very funny cousin," Tim gently slugged Jacob in the shoulder.

"Hey, lumberjack, watch it. I'm a professional."

"Oh, we can solve the superiority question of brains over brawn after dinner with a friendly game of pool."

"You're on, cuz," Jacob returned.

Enid started up the stairs while the men were still bantering back and forth. Mally was sitting on the sofa. She was dressed in gray Gap sweatpants and an oversized t-shirt. True to Mally-style, she looked as if she'd stepped out of a magazine. Her elegance was effortless. Although still pale she looked rested and relaxed.

"Hi," Enid said quietly. She didn't know what else to say so she took her mom's advice and walked over and gave Mally a hug.

"Hi yourself," Mally replied warmly, "Are you ready for a Tim-cooked meal?" her eyes twinkled in the Brown family tradition.

"I hope you've taught him something in the last few years because the last time he cooked for us it was over a fire on one of our famous summer horse campouts. Wieners and beans, if I recall."

Mally giggled in remembrance. "We were outlaws in hiding. I don't think we slept much either."

"No we didn't. It had something to do with a rain storm and having set our tent up too close to the river."

"Sounds like an interesting story," interrupted Jacob. "I think I remember this one. Didn't it end up with the three of you receiving a famous Uncle Ted lecture on the dangers of flash floods or something like that?"

"How did you know?" queried Tim.

125

"I confess," said Mally, "I used our adventures to impress my older, good-looking cousin."

"Now some things are beginning to make sense," laughed Tim. "I just thought Jacob was a good reader of the human psyche. I didn't realize one of the Musketeers broke the silence code! Enid, what was the penalty for snitching, do you remember?"

"If I recall it had something to do with cleaning tack for a month."

"Lucky for you, Mrs. Lewes, I don't have any tack left. But I think Enid might have some dirty tack by now for you to pay your dues on."

"As a matter of fact, I do," teased Enid, "and it's quite dirty already."

"Alright, alright, I give. I'll be out Monday morning to pay my debt to society."

"No, Mally, it's all right. I was just teasing. You don't really have to clean my tack," Enid said.

"But I will be out Monday morning."

Enid looked at Tim.

"We've talked, E, it's fine. Just no lifting or sweeping or riding for a couple of weeks yet."

"I guess that leaves the tack," smiled Enid.

"At one point the real Three Musketeers expanded their ranks to four you know," Jacob interjected, "but, before considering my application I was wondering if being a member means taking a vow of starvation?"

"At least someone is looking forward to experiencing Chef Tim's famous Swedish meatballs and rice. Dinner is served."

The meal was enjoyable and tasty. Enid had to concede to Tim that his culinary skills had improved with marriage.

Going Home

After the dishes were loaded up in the washer, the boys retreated to the basement for the promised pool game. Enid and Mally used the time to catch up on the last three years. Enid told of how she got a job at the bank and how her natural problem solving skills and risk taking attitude served her well in promotions. The freedom she enjoyed being single helped her to be able to work overtime and take extra courses that also contributed to her meteoric rise in the corporate ranks. Mally shared about time spent in the barn with Meredith and seeing Homebody, Homemaker and Home Hunter develop. Enid couldn't help feeling a jealousy rise in her. Mally had seen her mom and spent time at Homestead Farms over the last three years that were lost to Enid forever.

Enid distracted herself from introspection by asking lots of questions about the Young Guns previous training and Mally's impressions of them. Talking of horses was common ground that had been tread on for years, and the two slipped into the comfortable companionship they had shared for most of their lives. When the guys returned upstairs Jacob looked crestfallen. It seemed the lumberjack had beaten the vet.

"One for the west," piped up Tim.

"More like three games to none," moaned Jacob. "Why don't we play something the girls can join in on. You don't happen to have Scrabble do you?" Jacob winked at Enid.

"Of course, E and I used to play all the time," piped in Mally, "I'll get it."

"We can do this two ways. The Browns against the outsiders or the married against the single," Tim challenged.

"What God has put together we better not get in

between," Jacob boomed out sounding like a preacher from television.

"Okay then, bring it on." Tim was having way too much fun with Jacob included in the ranks.

Enid and Jacob's combined score was 598, the Brown's, 341. Jacob smirked, delighting in the victory.

"Enid, you brought a ringer into the house. I can't believe it," Mally acted hurt.

"I came for dinner and quiet conversation. I could see that wasn't going to happen with the guys sparring for dominance non-stop." She rolled her eyes like a child. "Boys!"

"Yeah, boys!" Mally linked her arm with Enid's. "We're going in the kitchen for dessert."

"Not without us," whined Tim.

The evening culminated over coffee, hot caramel pudding and Hagen Das Vanilla Ice Cream. By the time the last cup of coffee was finished up it was late. As Enid and Jacob made their way to the door, Mally asked about church.

"You'll be there, right E?" Mally asked.

Enid hesitated. Mally's eyes were peering out their own version of the SOS. Enid had already started the journey back. She had shed too many tears. She had faced too many fears to quit the journey now. With determination she took in a breath. Equal parts of fear and hope were wrestling for dominance. Enid cast her vote on hope's side.

"Yeah, I'll be there," Enid hugged Mally.

Tim gave Enid a hug goodnight. He whispered in her ear, "Thanks, E. I love you."

Fearing that any spoken word would release a wave of emotion, Enid could only squeeze her hug a little tighter in reply. It was enough.

Once outside in the fresh air Enid regained control over

Going Home

the ability of speech. She quickly made another decision. "Would you and Dr. Brown like to come for lunch after church?"

"Are you sure you're up to it?" Jacob inquired. "You have a lot on your plate as it is. Maybe we could bring lunch."

"No!" it slipped out louder than Enid had planned, "I mean Dr. Brown has already brought over Chinese and pizza. I think Mom and I can put lunch together." Enid smiled, "You can be my motivation to actually do some housework."

"I'll check with Uncle Ted but I'm sure our calendars are clear. I'm on call this Sunday so I'll travel with my pager."

"No problem. Phone me tomorrow."

"You got it, good night."

"Good night Jacob. And thanks for the great scrabble game. 'Cyclones,' double triple word combo with 50 bonus points for a total of 146. You can be my partner anytime."

Enid drove home without the aid of music. The reverberations of good-humored bantering were music enough to chase away any thoughts of despair.

Chapter Seventeen

Saturday sped by like the speed of sound. The Pony club was set to go to Victoria next week for the quiz rally. Enid wasn't required to go as enough parents had already signed up as volunteer helpers and drivers. The kids seemed well prepared for the various tasks they would face. Enid had set up a blind bag test for them. She put various pieces of tack in the bag and the kids had to identify it by feel only. The kids loved it and rose to the challenge.

Enid took her mom to the nursery where they picked up a couple of flats of early petunias and violets to fill in the bare spots of the front garden bed. They also picked up some groceries for the following week.

Enid worked the Young Guns in the afternoon. She was pleased with the progress being made in each of the their training and fitness. Before she knew where the time went, evening chores were upon her. She hummed and whistled as she fed each horse and pony. She gave Queenie some extra attention. The mare loved to be brushed. As Enid scratched the mare's shoulders with the currycomb, Queenie groaned in delight. Enid finished up and headed for the house. She caught her mom in the kitchen.

"Hey, I thought we agreed to prepare tomorrow's lunch together?" Enid scolded.

"I'm okay. I just wanted to make a cake," Meredith gave her the look, "I'm not a baby you know."

"Oh, I know that, but you are stubborn and you don't listen to Dr. Nichol. Besides, I already broke protocol by taking you shopping this afternoon. Do you want to get me into trouble?" With her hands on her hips Enid returned the look.

Meredith laughed, "Do I really look like that?"

"If I look seriously serious, then yes. Does it put fear in your little heart? Then yes," Enid shook her arms out and did facial contortions. "I better not overuse those muscles. I might actually have kids of my own one day and need them."

"Very funny, E." Meredith threw a kitchen towel her way.

Meredith and Enid enjoyed a quiet dinner together. While Enid was cleaning up the dishes, the phone rang. Meredith answered it and was pleased to hear her son, Mike, on the other end of the line.

"Oh, Mike that would be wonderful. Yes, honey all is well. Enid's been a real help. No, I don't think so. Okay, I look forward to it. Love you too." Meredith hung up the phone, a bright smile lighting up her face.

"What's up, Mom?"

"Mike, Elizabeth and the kids are coming up next weekend. Elizabeth went to her father and demanded that he give Mike a long weekend off so he could come and visit

Going Home

his injured mom. She's quite a girl. I guess she put it in such terms that her dad couldn't refuse. I can't wait to see the twins. They'll be here!"

"That's great! I haven't seen them since Christmas." Enid was looking forward to seeing her niece and nephew, her brother, however, was another story.

"The rooms should be ready. I'll double check them on Monday," Meredith said, mostly to herself.

"Mom, I'll check the rooms and if there is any fixing up to do I will do it. You listen to the doctor's orders and stay off you feet," Enid said firmly. She softened her tone, "Would you like some tea or something before bed?"

"Sure, honey, thanks."

~

Sunday morning Enid woke up an hour earlier than usual. She quietly descended the stairs. She was glad that her mom was still sleeping. Enid put the coffee on and then headed out to the barn. All was well, but by the time she got back into the house she found her mom in the kitchen. She had made porridge and was just finishing up the preparations for lunch. Enid started to give her the look.

Meredith simply said, "You can't keep a good woman down."

Enid could only smile and agreed.

The drive to church felt different from last week, less apprehension was running in Enid's veins. Her mom and Mally would surely take most of the congregation's attention. Unlike last week Enid and Meredith entered the building before the music started. Mr. and Mrs. McGregor were their usual bubbly and friendly selves. They gave each of the Taylor women their famous hug. Enid could return it this week without the worry of erupting all over them. She breathed a sigh of relief and escorted her mom to a chair near the back where she had room to put her leg up.

The church was nearly full when Mally and Tim entered. People kept their distance to a degree, letting them get settled. Dr. Brown came in after them accompanied by Jacob. Jacob left his Uncle and came to sit with Enid.

"Good morning Mrs. Taylor, Enid" he said.

"Good morning Jacob," Meredith replied.

"Hi Jacob. You could have sat with your uncle if you wanted to," Enid pointed out.

"I know but two good looking, eligible women, such as yourselves should not be left unescorted, especially when you've invited me for lunch." He grinned broadly. "I want to make sure you don't duck out early and forget about us."

Meredith laughed and drew the attention of several people including Ted Brown. Their eyes met and Enid could feel the warmth pass between them. She looked away smiling to herself. Spring fever was indeed in the air.

The worship team opened the service with a favorite old song. Everyone got to their feet and clapped along. Everyone but Enid. She stayed seated with her mom. Fear won the first round. Jacob, however, stood and joined in adding his strong tenor voice with the congregation.

The youth pastor, Lee Shepherd, who was new since January, opened in prayer and greeted everyone. The congregation all clapped for Meredith's return. The worship leader then led in a song that Enid didn't know. Meredith leaned over to her daughter. "This is my new favorite song."

Enid smiled politely in response. She tried to distract herself from the words and melody but they penetrated to the deep empty place left after shedding gallons of tears since she had returned home.

Going Home

Out of the corner of her eye she saw Mally and Tim rise to their feet. They raised their hands to the sky with tears streaming down their faces. The song continued and the beat of the drums resounded with the pounding of Enid's heart.

You are the hope living in us;
You are the rock in whom we trust;

As the worship leader started to sing it the second time through a voice whispered deep in Enid's soul. "Jesus, Jesus, Jesus," was all it said. Enid glimpsed up at Mally. Her face radiated peace and hope through the tears and obvious pain. Tim was smiling with angelic likeness as his arms were raised to the roof. Jacob's face shone with the moisture of teary cheeks, he looked peaceful. Others in the room, that Enid knew had suffered pain and sorrow, joined in with conviction, singing of Jesus as the hope and the light. It struck Enid that heaven was the source of hope, heaven was the source of light and it came to earth in the form of Jesus. She had always loved Jesus.

The rest of the song service was lost on her. She was reminded of times from her childhood when she had envisioned Jesus in the barn. After all, he was born in a barn wasn't he? Enid had spent a lot of time as a child and a teenager telling Jesus everything. Her father had told her she had a great prayer life but Enid never thought of it as prayer. It was just talking to her friend. In her late teens she was very busy working on her A rating and teaching pony club. She missed quite a few weekends and it affected her relationship with God and her church family. She stopped growing. She knew there was more. She saw it emerging out of people she loved: Mally, Tim, Lucy, her parents. She had felt closer to Mike then. He had stopped going to church and Enid felt validated in her choice to pursue her career over the church's agenda.

Before Enid realized, Pastor Dave was standing behind the pulpit and the musicians were sitting down. "Today's scripture comes from the letter to the Hebrews, Chapter Four, starting in verse one. I'm reading from the Message Bible: 'For as long then, as that promise of resting in him pulls us on to God's goal for us, we need to be careful that we're not disqualified. We received the promises as those people in the wilderness, but the promises didn't do them a bit of good because they didn't receive the promises with faith. If we believe, though, we'll experience that state of resting. But not if we don't have faith.' Skip down to verse 9. 'The promise of "arrival" and "rest" is still there for God's people. God himself is at rest. And at the end of the journey we'll surely rest with God. So let's keep at it and eventually arrive at the place of rest, not drop out through some sort of disobedience. God means what he says. What he says goes. His powerful Word is as sharp as a surgeon's scalpel, cutting through everything, whether doubt or defense, laying us open to listen and obey. Nothing and no one is impervious to God's Word. We can't get away from it—no matter what.'"

The Word penetrated Enid's heart. The last few days she had experienced a glimmer of peace and rest that she hadn't known for a very long time, longer than before her dad's death. She knew that she had walked away from Jesus, left him on a shelf to be picked up at a convenient time. When the accident happened, it was easy to blame it on God when, in reality, Enid feared that God was getting back at her because she had ignored him for so long. Jacob's story of making a decision to believe God pierced Enid's mind. She believed in God and in what Jesus did on the cross for her.

GOING HOME

She knew Jesus made access to God the Father possible but she had quit believing God. Mally and Tim believed God—that He was good and that He had the peace and hope they needed for the struggle to recover from the loss of their baby. Her mom, Dr. Brown, Lucy—they hadn't fallen apart or run away from God because of tragedy.

"As most of you know Tim and Mally Lewes lost their unborn child last Sunday morning. They've requested that the elder's pray for them during this difficult time." Pastor Dave's voice cut into Enid's thoughts.

Tim and Mally stood up. They walked, arm in arm toward the front of the church. Pastor Dave and his wife Carol, Dr. Brown and others met them there. They surrounded them protectively. Dr. Brown lovingly put his hands on Tim and Mally touching their heads. Others joined him. The people laying their hands on Tim and Mally mesmerized Enid. She had seen this numerous times, even experienced it, but today it seemed different, it seemed powerful. Enid could hear Mally's quiet sobs. She looked at her mom. Meredith's eyes were closed and her right hand was extended toward the couple. Her lips were moving in silent prayer. The worship team had returned to the platform. They sang of the hope found only in Christ. Enid felt a stirring in her spirit. She felt compelled to get up or bow down or to go to the altar, to talk to someone but she just couldn't. She sat frozen in her chair until it was time to go. Her mom finally stood up. Enid was jarred out of her thoughts. Dr. Brown walked over taking Meredith's hand.

"Merry, it's good to see you back in church."

"I was only gone one Sunday, Ted." Meredith blushed.

"I know, but I missed you."

Enid was still too caught up in her own thoughts to interject anything.

"Enid."

She looked at Dr. Brown, "Yes?"

"Would you mind if your mom came with me back to the farm? It seems Jacob was hoping for a ride in a certain sports car."

"That's fine." Enid was somewhat relieved. She knew Jacob would respect her privacy of thought.

Jacob escorted her to the Crossfire. Enid got behind the wheel and waited for him to fold into the passenger seat. "Do you mind if we wait for a minute?" Enid asked quietly.

"Sure, you're driving," Jacob said lightly.

"I really want to see Mally," Enid cut it short. She didn't want to cry today.

"No problem," came the amicable reply.

Enid sat still with her hands at the ten and two positions on the steering wheel. She looked like a racecar driver waiting for the green flag. Jacob could feel a tension, electricity, fill the automobile.

After about two minutes Tim and Mally made their way down the stairs. They were alone hand in hand, their faces shining, freshly washed in tears. Enid watched them walk over to the little blue Mazda 3. Before they reached it, Enid climbed out of her car and walked hurriedly over to Mally.

"Mal," she called out.

Mally turned. Enid jogged the rest of the way right into her friend's open arms. They stood entwined as one for a minute.

"Jesus," Enid started, "heal my friend. Heal my friend."

Mally tightened her grip. "Jesus," she wept, "heal my friend, too. Heal my friend."

Going Home

Enid couldn't hold the tears back anymore. But the tears felt different from any she had ever cried. They didn't burn her face as they made their way down. They were cool, refreshing, like standing under a soft shower in the tropics. Not cold and harsh, not hot and burning, but cool, refreshing. Enid didn't sob from her gut like in the tack room. She breathed in deep even breaths, relaxed, at peace.

"Thank you, E, your prayer means more to me than you know."

"Same to you, Mal," Enid released her friend and looked into her beautiful face. "I'll never leave you again," Enid added strongly.

"E, you may have tried to leave me but you didn't. You don't have the power to. You are knit on my heart, in my soul, so close not even death can separate us." Mally's voice was strong, passionate. "You're my kindred spirit."

Enid smiled. She hadn't thought of that before. She thought she had the power to choose. She did, but only for herself, not for anyone else. She had lived for so long denying that for her dad and her horse. She hadn't let the bonds have a voice. A wave of reconciliation swept over her. Her mind, her will, her emotions, so long separated into neat little compartments, never allowed an audience together with her spirit, were suddenly and firmly meshed together. She felt a literal jolt of electricity run from her inner core out through all her extremities. It was like she had been living in a one-dimensional world. Flat. Grey scale. She was now transported to three or more dimensions and full techni-color. Look out Dorothy! Enid was now in Oz, and unlike her predecessor, this was home and she had no desire to leave.

"Mally, I'm home. I'm really home," Enid was beaming.

Mally reached out to Tim who was standing a step away.

He came and joined the circle. Enid squeezed him so hard he thought he was going to be bruised for a week.

"Tim, I'm sorry for all the pain I've caused you. Please forgive me."

"E, there's nothing to forgive. I need to ask your forgiveness. I said such stupid things to you when you lost your dad and Home Boy. I was so unfeeling, so uncompassionate. I didn't know the pain, the hurt, or the doubt you went through. I do now," he broke. "If it hadn't been for Mally, Dad Brown, Pastor Dave, your mom and Jacob, I don't know where I'd be. They helped me see that it wasn't anything we did wrong. God wasn't punishing us for anything. My hope is not attached to how good life is. It's anchored in who Jesus is. I'm so sorry I wasn't there for you, E, I'm so sorry."

Enid squeezed him harder. "It's all good now," she said.

Jacob walked over to the group. "I know the verdict is still out on admitting the fourth musketeer but I was wondering if I could get some of that."

The friends laughed and opened their arms to enlarge the circle. Jacob joined them linking his arms with Enid and Tim. They stood there for few minutes. As each second passed it seemed to strengthen the bond between the young people. Not only were they linked arm in arm, but heart to heart and spirit-to-spirit as well.

"Jacob, thank you for your wisdom and the courage to share your story with us," Tim said. "I married into the right family that's for sure."

Enid looked up at Jacob. He remained the same—peaceful, sure, and steady. Enid had a hard time picturing him ever having doubt, ever being broken. He caught her eye. They lit up like his uncles. *He knows*, Enid thought, *he knows what's happened in me*. She wasn't sure if she even

Going Home

knew what had happened but she returned his look with a steady, peace-filled gaze.

"We better let you two go," Mally broke in. "Shouldn't leave my dad alone with your mom for too long."

Enid laughed, "You don't really mind, do you?"

"Not if you don't." Mally chimed.

"You're right, we should go." Enid looked at Jacob with a twinkle in her eye. "You wouldn't mind driving would you, Jacob?"

"Oh, you could twist my arm," was the enthusiastic reply.

He quickly made his way to the driver's side of the sleek automobile. Enid sat in the unusual position in the passenger seat. As Jacob maneuvered the attractive vehicle over the now familiar roads to Homestead Farm, Enid relaxed back into the leather and closed her eyes. She wasn't tired, she just needed to be in a space without distraction. She breathed in and out consciously. It felt like the air was rarified. She felt in a different dimension. Without realizing it she let out a contented sigh.

"Enid," a voice interjected.

She opened her eyes and looked at Jacob. "Did I say that out loud?" she asked wistfully.

"You didn't really say anything but you do sound as if you are content, at peace even."

"I think I'm beginning to see, in a small way, the difference you were talking about between believing God and believing in God. I've always loved Jesus, have always believed in what he did on the cross. I know that Heaven exists, it's just that I've buried that part of my life for a long time."

She paused, "I see now that it was the wrong choice. What I ran from during the most painful time in my life is what I should have run to—the throne of my Father in heaven. I blamed him when I really should have run to him—he's the only hope, the only light. I'm not really sure how to start over, how to reboot that part of my life. I just know that I can't hold my God at bay any longer." She looked over at Jacob. "I feel free, I can't explain it. Light. Sorrow seems to be gone. I feel hope for the future. I haven't felt hope in such a long time. Purpose too. I'm rambling, sorry."

"Don't be sorry," Jacob said. "I'm so happy for you, Enid. I knew you would come through. You have an inner strength that makes it easy for you to do so much on your own but, eventually, we all have to come to the end of ourselves. You're lucky to have been brought up in a Christian home. All the times you've heard a sermon or read the Bible, it's all in there, lying dormant. And now it will come back out and feed you. Just open the Word of God and ask him to reveal himself to you. It won't matter what you read, he'll quicken it to you. After all, it is alive."

Jacob pulled up to the house and turned off the purring engine. "Thanks for letting me drive your car. It was as good as I thought it would be, though next time I'd like to bring it up the road to Mt. Washington and give the suspension a real workout."

"We'll see about that," Enid said.

Meredith and Ted were in the kitchen sitting at the table enjoying a cup of coffee when Jacob and Enid arrived. "Hey, what took you two?" Meredith asked.

"I needed to see Mal," Enid said.

"Is everything all right?" her mom asked.

"Yes, everything's fine, Mom."

Enid and Meredith laid out the lunch. Jacob and Ted each complimented the cooks as they enjoyed the Greek

Going Home

Pasta Salad, oven fried chicken and wild rice. Meredith's chocolate cake topped off the meal. Jacob couldn't resist a second piece. After the dishes were cleared up they exchanged riotous laughter and teasing over a game of Mexican Train dominoes. Jacob lost soundly as he ate the blank tile for 50 negative points six times out of the nine rounds. Meredith on the other hand, won by over 100 points.

"Do you think we could partner up, Enid, and challenge your mom and my uncle to Scrabble?"

"We could but you should know one thing. My mom taught me how to play and constantly reminds me of all those non-descript two and three letter words."

"Ah, well, then. I think I've endured enough humiliation for one day."

"I'm sorry Jacob. I guess it was just my lucky day," Meredith said in her defense.

"Now Jacob, you can't win all the time," his uncle teased. "He was top of his class in Vet School, Merry, so don't feel too sorry for him."

"I really should go out and do evening chores." Enid broke in, "How time flies when you're having fun," she added cheerfully.

"I'll come with you, E," said Jacob.

With Jacob's knowledgeable help the chores went smoothly and quickly. After the last piece of hay was swept up and the broom put away Enid led Jacob to Queenie's stall. They lingered at her door. Jacob's knowledgeable eyes surveyed her in all her growing glory.

"She looks great as broodmares go." Jacob observed. "You should see some of the heartbreak cases I've dealt with."

"My mom would starve herself before she'd let the horses go one night without food. Especially Queenie."

143

At the mention of her name the rotund mare came to the door pushing her face toward Enid. She was compelled to rub the spot between her huge liquid eyes. The mare groaned contentedly.

"Some days it must be tough to be a vet. I've never really thought beyond the routine exams and pregnancy checks. Well, I did once, but…" Enid paused.

"They had to winch Home Boy out of the trailer. They didn't know how badly he was hurt. He was always calm in any situation. He saved me many times on the cross-country field and in the jumper ring because of his ability to read a situation and override my bad decisions. He just let them do what they had to do. When he was free from the wreckage he tried to get up. That's when it became clear that his near front leg was cut so deeply that it was barely attached. They put him down there on the side of the road.

"The vet had to make that decision alone. My dad was dead, my mom was out and I was unreachable. The vet tried to talk to me on and off for two months after the accident. I just couldn't talk to him. I hated him for killing my horse, for making that decision that should have been mine. The poor man, I never gave him the benefit of a second thought about his responsibility, his feelings."

Jacob had put his arm around Enid supporting her, comforting her as she opened up. She looked up at him, thankful for the safety, the surety he gave her. "Wow, I bet you never had a clue what you were in for when you asked to share my table on that ferry," Enid laughed weakly.

"No, I didn't, but I'm not complaining."

They turned out the lights and made their way back up to the house.

Chapter Eighteen

The week flew by. Mally came out in the mornings to feed. She was under strict instructions and Enid made sure she followed her husband's and her doctor's orders. After feeding, she came in for coffee or hot chocolate and then Enid chased her home. Mally wanted to stay and watch Enid ride but each day she reluctantly left for home as Enid headed back to the barn.

Enid was gaining strength and stamina in her riding and the Young Guns were all fitting up well. Their coats were now shiny and clean. Home Hunter was loping around the 3' courses like an old campaigner. Enid hoped that the experience of being in a strange stall and jumping in a strange ring with the myriad of distractions around him would not put him off his game next week. Enid had taken him out and ridden him with Leonora to simulate a bit of a show like atmosphere. He never put a foot wrong. Enid's expectations for the gray soared.

Homebody was taking to regular work like a duck to

water. He complained every time Enid took Home Hunter or Homemaker out of their stalls. He eagerly jumped everything Enid set. She kept the height at 3'3, knowing the move up to 3'6" wasn't going to be an issue for the big bay.

Homemaker was getting bored on the lunge line and Enid knew the time was approaching quickly for her to move on to the next stage of training—bearing the weight of a rider on her back and learning to submit to the pressure of legs and reins.

Her mom was mirroring the filly's impatience. Meredith was aching to get out to the barn. Her limited view from the house was not enough to satisfy her growing curiosity. On Tuesday, when she made Enid drive her down to watch the pony club lessons, Enid knew her mom was going to make it to the barn whether she or Dr. Nichol liked it or not.

By Wednesday, Enid felt ready to let her mom out of the house, and to climb on Homemaker's back for the first time. Dr. Brown had agreed to come over to help Meredith get down to the barn and to help Enid keep Meredith from doing too much. Ede was on board as well to help Enid with Homemaker.

The morning dawned gray and wet. Looking out at the steadily falling rain, Enid was thankful for the indoor riding arena. She made her way out to the barn and fed the horses. She gave Homemaker an extra scratch and looked forward to finally sitting on her back.

After breakfast was finished, Enid worked in the office. She was going over the pony club lessons when she heard a knock on the back door. It was the stroke of ten o'clock and Ede and Dr. Brown arrived as promised. She greeted them cheerfully.

Going Home

"Good morning, Ede, Dr. Brown," Enid said with enthusiasm.

"Good morning, E, and when do you think you can call me Ted?" Dr. Brown mused.

"Maybe when I'm 40," teased Enid. "I think you'll always be Dr. Brown to me."

Ede chirped in, "Are you excited to get on that mare, Enid?"

"Well, I'm certainly curious," came the answer.

"I'm excited!" interjected Meredith. "Excited to get out of the house and walk down to the barn."

"Change of plans, Merry," Ted stated authoritatively, "I'm driving you down to the barn. It's raining and the walk will be too slippery for crutches."

Meredith started to protest but Ted cut her short. "No discussion." Meredith clapped her jaw shut.

Enid looked at Ted with new respect. He could handle her mom. She turned her attention to Ede. "Let's go and get the filly ready now. Mom, you and Dr... I mean Ted, can come in about 15 minutes." Enid and Ede left for the barn.

"I thought, perhaps, that Ada would be with you."

"She doesn't know I'm here. On Wednesday mornings she goes with other home-schooled kids for gym class at the rec center."

Homemaker nickered as the barn door opened. Enid usually worked her first so she was waiting. On cue, Homebody whinnied his objections when the mare walked to the crosstie area. Between Ede and Enid the mare was tacked up and led to the arena by the time Ted and Meredith appeared.

"Oh, baby girl, look at you all grown-up," crooned

Meredith as she hobbled over to the bleachers. Ted helped her up.

"I'm going to lunge her first," Enid informed her audience.

The mare moved out to the end of the line like a pro. She walked sedately around, paying attention to Enid's every move. When she moved up to trot, the mare floated around the circle, flicking her hooves out in front like a ballet dancer.

"E, her gait is improved. Good job, honey."

"She's in better shape than she was a couple of weeks ago. Fitness helps."

Homemaker cantered away quietly as Enid kissed to the filly. After a few rounds, Enid halted the mare and changed directions. Going to the right, the mare was not as consistent about staying out to the end of the line but horses, like people, are usually one-sided.

After the canter to the right Enid brought the mare in and had Ede come into the center. With Ede at the mare's head Enid brought the mounting block to the mare's left side. She stood up on it and petted Homemaker's neck. The filly's ears were turned in Enid's direction. Her eye was attentive to what Enid was doing. Enid stepped off the stool and then back up again talking to the mare in a singsong voice and scratching her shoulder and neck. After five times the mare was relaxed and not so keyed onto what Enid was doing. Enid then put both arms over the saddle and rubbed the other side of the mare. Homemaker was enjoying the attention and didn't seem too concerned with what her funny human friend was doing.

Enid then leaned her weight over the saddle. The mare braced her feet under herself and skirted away a bit but Enid

Going Home

continued to lie over the saddle. She slid down and moved the mounting block back to the mare's side. She draped her body over the saddle again and asked Ede to move the mare around the arena. Homemaker walked away, looking drunk under the influence of Enid's body flopped over the saddle but she raised no other objections. Her gait eventually smoothed out and Ede halted the mare. Enid slipped down once more and made much of the mare telling her how smart she was. She gave her some treats and rubbed her face.

The three of them made their way back to the mounting block and this time Enid put her foot in the stirrup. She lightly and quickly mounted the mare. Homemaker raised her head as her back sunk down. Ede was talking to her and holding on to the bridle. The mare did a 360-degree circle around Ede while Enid patted her neck and talked to her. After a few revolutions the mare stopped with her legs splayed out under her like Bambi on ice. Enid gave her a moment to assess the situation. The mare snorted out a horse sigh and then violently shook like a dog after a bath. Enid relaxed and let her body move with the horse. Homemaker ended up standing properly under herself. Enid asked Ede to lead the mare around. Homemaker followed Ede but every once in a while tried to look up to see what Enid was doing. Enid remained relaxed becoming one with the horse. Soon Homemaker became used to the extra burden on her back and followed Ede around patiently. Enid asked Ede to halt the mare and then to lunge her as before. The mare willingly went back around the circle to the left. Ede increased the pace to the trot. Homemaker complied not giving her passenger much thought. Ede asked the mare to walk and then to halt. Homemaker enjoyed all the attention she was receiving from Ede on the ground and from Enid on her back. They turned the mare around and proceeded to trot in the other direction. Enid was happy with the progress for the first lesson. She slipped off the mare's back and treated her like a queen.

"What a smart girl, you are," came the singsong voice Homemaker knew and loved. Enid scratched her in all the right places. She undid the saddle and gave her back a good rub, looking out for any bumps or rubs that weren't there before.

"E, you've done a wonderful job. Thank you, honey," Meredith said. "She sure is like her momma," she added proudly.

"Yes, she is," said Enid contentedly. "It's too bad you're selling out, Mom. You finally bred Queenie's replacement."

"You're selling, Mrs. Taylor?" Ede inquired.

"Oh, Mom, I'm sorry," Enid panicked.

"No, Ede, I'm not selling, not yet anyway. But I am thinking about it. Please don't panic. I'll officially let you know if there's any change. There's no need to move," Meredith responded calmly and professionally.

"Ada would be heartbroken to move. She loves it here. We all do. Hillary and Amelia's moms were asking me about board. I hope you don't mind but I told them how much I was paying."

"Of course not. It's not a secret. The rates are posted for all to see."

"They were asking about boarding?" Enid interrupted. "Aren't they happy at Tina Crooms'?"

"Oh they're happy enough. I think they're just comparing. You know how it is."

Enid knew. The horse business was very competitive. It would be interesting to see the girls at the horse show.

Going Home

They may be her pony club students but they rode with Mrs. Crooms. They were her riding students.

"Is Bekah at home?" Enid asked.

"She just got back from California," Ted jumped in. "I'm sure you'll see her at the show next week."

"Well, Homemaker, you sweetie, you'll be staying in your nice familiar stall next week but your buddies will travel to the show so I better get on with my morning routine."

The entourage escorted the mare back to the crossties. Ede brushed her and put her away while Enid got Home Hunter out.

"Are you staying down, Mom, or are you too tired?"

"I really want to see you ride the boys."

"Ted? Are you okay or do you have to leave?"

"I'm fine, I took the whole day off. It's great to have some help now. I think I could get used to having regular days off." He smiled flashing his bright eyes.

"Okay, but I'll be at least another hour."

Enid put Home Hunter through his paces, much to her mother's delight. The gray gelding had really improved since Enid started to ride him. His fitness was enhanced but it was the way he was jumping that got the applause from Meredith.

"E, you have no idea what good it does me to see you riding but not only that! The exercises you've set up for Home Hunter have improved his way of moving. Wow! I see what you were talking about. He is a hunter."

"He's more than a hunter, Mom. He's first class." Enid smiled giving her face muscles another exercise.

Ede came and took Home Hunter from Enid. Now she could get to the main man. Homebody was pawing at his door. He knew what time it was. Enid reset the jumps before she got the gelding. She used the same figure eight hunter course as for Home Hunter but raised the jumps.

When Enid led the big gelding in Meredith gasped. "E, what have you done to my boy?"

Enid smiled. She knew her mom was impressed with how Homebody looked. She had spent a lot of elbow grease on the gelding's coat over the last couple of weeks.

"Therapy, Mom, lots of therapy."

"I remember Bo Jangles always looked the best when Mally was going through some tough stuff," Ted smiled.

"'The outside of a horse is good for the inside of a man' so the old adage goes," quoted Meredith. "I think it would be more accurate to say 'inside of a teenage girl.'"

"Too true, Merry," agreed Ted.

Enid began to warm the gelding up. She used the same system that Ruth demonstrated in the D2 pony club lesson, planned and precise. Her mom had drilled it into her since she first put a leg over Davy Crockett. The gelding knew the routine and began to anticipate the next move so Enid started to mix it up a bit with leg yield, shoulder-in and halt transitions. Homebody sharpened up in his attention so that by the time they were cantering Enid could compress or lengthen his stride at will. She pointed him to the first line of jumps: a 3' vertical 58 feet to a 3'3" oxer. The gelding effortlessly loped down and folded over the vertical. Enid kept his canter stride short to fit in the five strides between the fences. He rounded over the oxer, tucking his knees up square to his cheeks. On the landing side he picked up his canter and carried on in rhythm to the diagonal line. He cleared the two 3'3" verticals and neatly did a flying lead change in the corner before heading for the last line of fences. The pair of oxers was no contest for the gelding's athletic prowess. He left Enid

Going Home

breathless, his presence and power constantly impressed her. She pulled the gelding up in front of the bleachers.

"Wow," was all Ede could say.

Meredith had a hint of tears in the corner of her eyes. "I knew he was good but I didn't really know he was that good. Even with his success last year he showed talent but not the raw power I just saw. He's really matured over the winter."

"E," Ted also seemed emotional, "It's so good to see you in the saddle again. Watching you with the filly and the young guy was one thing, but seeing you on this gelding, it brings back so many memories," he paused, "good memories."

"He is rather special, isn't he?" Enid said proudly, patting the gelding.

Ede helped Enid put the gelding away and clean up while her mom and Ted returned to the house to make coffee.

Chapter Nineteen

The rest of the week flew by with Pony Club lessons, continued training of the Young Guns, and the day-to-day responsibilities 11 horses bring. It wasn't until Friday night that Enid had any time to talk to her mom about the responses she had received from the Internet ads for the Young Guns.

"Mom, there's been quite a bit of interest from the ads I put on the Internet."

"Really, E, from who? Where are they from? Who are they interested in? How much did you advertise them for anyway?" Meredith shot the questions out faster than a Gatlin gun.

"Whoa, whoa, not so fast," protested Enid. "One question at a time."

"E, don't tease me," pouted her mother. "Tell me what you know."

"Okay, first of all a family from California is interested in all three horses. It seems money is no object and they'll

155

be here next weekend on a horse-hunting trip. I've told them about the show and they're going to try to make it to see the boys go. Homemaker is the lowest on their list, as she isn't really going yet. I've asked $60,000 for Homebody and $30,000 for Home Hunter. Right now Homemaker is $20,000 but that'll go up as her training continues," Enid stopped because she thought her mom was about to faint.

"Sixty… thousand? Dollars?" Meredith grabbed her throat. "E, what have you done? No one will pay that for Homebody. I know he's good, but sixty thousand?"

"Mom, I did my research on the Internet. If anything I asked too little. He has a good show record, he's young, and he's still eligible for certain Hunter Divisions since he hasn't been shown in A rated shows. You saw him. He's exceptional. Mom, don't forget we were offered $50,000 for Home Boy when we won the 4'6" Jumper Championship at Thunderbird. That was 4 years ago. The market is still there. And besides," Enid paused, "Homebody is better than Home Boy."

Enid didn't think her mom's eyes could get bigger but they did. "Do you really think so, E?" gasped her mom.

"I know so. His raw power is indescribable. Plus he compresses his huge stride easily. Home Boy wasn't as handy. Mom, if he sold, I should think most of your cash flow problems would be gone."

"It would help." Her mom sounded unsure. Enid was puzzled. Her mom looked at her thoughtfully. "I wish I didn't have to sell any horses to strangers." Meredith took a breath. "It's not just the money, E. I feel like this part of my life is waning. It's like a death of sorts. I'll always love horses and it will be extremely hard to see any of them sold," Meredith

Going Home

got quiet. "I don't know what I'll do once I'm back on my feet and you go back to Vancouver."

"I'll make sure the work is covered, I promise." Enid reached out to her mom. "It's okay, Mom. You've dedicated so much time and effort into this thing and most of it was for me. Thank you from the bottom of my heart. I wouldn't have traded my childhood with anyone else."

Meredith hugged her daughter. "I'm glad, E," she sighed, "I know you don't like it when I say this but you do have a gift with horses. That was evident to everyone watching the other day."

"I can't deny that the last week has been the best one for a very long time. I feel more at home and at peace than I have since even before the accident. I've been reading the Bible again, mostly the Psalms. It's really helped me to see that God doesn't change, that He is good and faithful and that I don't need to get all the answers down here."

"I'm glad to hear that, E. I lived in the Psalms the first year after your dad died. They were a real comfort." Meredith began to laugh quietly to herself.

"What?" Enid prodded.

"Oh, I was just remembering the night I took the Bible out to the furthest corner of the property and yelled and screamed God's word right back at Him. Boy did that feel good!"

"Honey," this time Meredith took her daughter's hand, "consider your future, too." She looked at Enid as only a mom can—deeply, knowingly, hauntingly.

"I am, Mom, believe me, I am."

Chapter Twenty

The Pony Clubbers returned victorious from Quiz Rally. Ada's D team, consisting of her, the twins and Ruth placed first. Ede was beaming when they came to the barn Saturday night to show Mr. Big the ribbon and give him some of the horse treats that Ada had won.

"I guess all my nagging wasn't in vain," Ede said.

"Congratulations!" Enid said enthusiastically. "Great job to everyone. How did the other teams do?"

"The two junior teams placed 2nd and 5th, the other D teams were 3rd and 6th, so overall a very successful day. Oh, I almost forgot, Ruth was the highest placed D overall."

"That's great! She's a good rider too, I wish her parents could buy her a horse."

"Enid, they can barely afford pony club on a borrowed pony. That's why she isn't going to the show next weekend. There just isn't money for anything extra. I think that's one reason she does so well in the Stable Management and Quiz. It's something she can study and pursue that doesn't cost anything but time. She did well last year at Rally too as a groom. She's a great kid."

"Do you think her parents would let her come out here on days other than pony club?"

"I don't know, you could always ask. What are you thinking?"

"Well, I need to find some help for my mom and I'm hoping to maybe help Ruth out as well."

"You know, Enid, Ada and I are willing to help too. We don't mind."

"Really? How about the evening feed, two times a week?"

"Done. Can we do Tuesdays and Thursdays?"

"Absolutely. What if we take off $50.00 a month for board? Does that sound fair?"

"No, that's not fair to you. Tell you what, I'll trade you for lessons."

"Ede, my friend, you have a deal."

Enid gave Leonora a lesson on Saturday afternoon and she actually got the pair over a 2'6" Hunter course. Joe was steady and willing, good qualities for a hunter. He would never be a 3'6" jumper but since Leonora had no such aspiration, the two of them were a perfect match.

"It's my professional opinion that you should enter the show next week and do the 2'6" Adult Amateur Hunter Division," Enid coached Leonora.

"I guess next week's show is as good as any other show," Leonora conceded.

"So you'll do it?"

"Actually, I've already entered. I decided to risk it after my second lesson."

Going Home

"What? Leonora, when were you going to let me in on it?" Enid laughed.

"Today."

"In that case I have another course or two for you to practice."

Later, when Enid entered the house a surprise was waiting for her. "Mal, Tim, how are you?"

"Great, E, we came to see if you would like to come out to a movie with us," Mally said cheerily.

"Oh, um, Mom, would you be okay if I went out?" Enid asked.

"Of course, E, Ted's coming over later with a DVD for us. Go out and have some fun."

"Okay, Mal. What time do you want me to meet you?"

"We were thinking the 7:40 movie at the mall."

"I'll meet you there, then."

After Mal and Tim left Enid had a shower and grabbed a quick bite to eat. With Ted coming over, Enid was glad to have somewhere to go. She wanted them to have as much space as possible.

The movie was a romantic comedy. Even though Enid felt somewhat like the third wheel, she determined to enjoy herself. Tim and Mal were great, just like old times and Enid recognized again that it was she who had left. She was grateful that she'd been given a second chance with her long time friends.

A coffee at the White Spot finished off the evening. As Enid drove home, she found herself actually looking forward to church in the morning. She had come a long way in a couple of weeks. Enid drove up to the house and parked. As she made her way to the back door she surprised her mom and Ted, catching them in a goodnight kiss. All were embarrassed and an awkward silence fell on the trio.

"Um, ah, excuse me." Enid smiled to herself and squeezed past the couple making it into her room in record time. Once inside the safety of her room she jumped onto her bed, buried her face in her pillow, and burst into hysterical laughter. She laughed until she was in tears. She didn't understand what was so funny but she couldn't stop the giggles.

The next morning at breakfast, Meredith couldn't stop the blush that rose on her cheek like the early morning sun. "E, about last night," her mom started to explain.

"Mom, please, you're a grown woman, so am I and so is Dr. Brown, I mean he's a man of course…" Enid turned her face away. The giggles were coming back.

"I, well, I mean, I'm sorry. You seemed so upset last night. I've hardly slept thinking about it. I heard you in your room. Honey, if this is too hard for you… I'll just tell Ted…"

Enid couldn't keep the gut wrenching giggles at bay any longer. They burst out of her in a rush. "I wasn't upset, Mom, I got the giggles so bad I thought I was going to explode in front of you two lovebirds," Enid laughed out loud. "I'm sorry, it was just so awkward." Enid had to break for the waves of laughter that were rolling out of her.

"You're not upset?" Meredith seemed unconvinced. The giggles kept Enid at a loss for coherent speech. She shook her head.

"You're okay with Ted and me? Even if we are no longer just friends?"

"Yes, Mom. I'm actually thrilled," speech returned, thankfully.

"Though I'll need a schedule of your 'intimate moments.'

Going Home

I don't want to interrupt you just when things are getting interesting." Some unfinished giggles escaped.

"I can't tell you how happy you've made me, E." Instead of laughter, tears emerged.

"Mom, don't cry," Enid urged. "Are you okay with you and Ted being more than friends? Did he make a move on you last night that you weren't expecting?"

Now the tears turned to giggles. "If anyone 'made a move' I did," Meredith confessed, "It was rather awkward, wasn't it?"

The Taylor women locked eyes for the first time that morning. They exploded into a torrent of giggles. The light mood and the radiant faces accompanied them to church. Ted was waiting outside, looking as nervous as a teenager about to meet the parents of his girlfriend for the first time. Enid walked right up to him and gave him a hug. When she let him go his face was trying to outshine his eyes. Enid looked from him to her mom and then left them standing there looking at each other. She entered the church by herself, confident and at peace.

Chapter Twenty-One

The week before the show was a hectic race against the march of Old Man Time. Enid had forgotten how much needed to be done to get ready. She was glad of Mally's help but she still had to chase her home every morning.

The daily routine kept the horses fed and clean. Enid had always been careful with her tack. She never let it get too dirty but before the show she wanted every nick and cranny free of dust, dirt, sweat and 'jockeys,' little bumps of greasy dirt that accumulate on the pieces of leather. Every waking moment was now filled up with the extra work so when Wednesday, May first arrived, she had completely forgotten that the vet was coming. She was setting up a new course when Jacob poked his head into the arena. He was in coveralls. That jogged the appointment out from under the pile of things on Enid's "to-do list."

"Jacob, I completely forgot you were coming this morning."

"That's okay, you're here."

Enid left the jumps and proceeded to help Jacob with the Young Guns. They each received their shots and had their teeth filed. Homemaker had to have two baby teeth removed. With all three having to be tranquilized Enid's plans of working them that morning went out the window. She hated to lose a day's work this close to the show.

"Well, at least I can say in all honesty that their shots and teeth are up to date when the Californians come to call."

"Are you showing the horses to prospective buyers this week, E?" Jacob asked.

"Yes, the Internet ads have created quite a bit of interest. The first people to come look in the flesh are from California. I think they're in the Vancouver area this week and are coming to the island for the weekend. I'm hoping to show Home Hunter and Homebody to them at the show."

"I'll remember that in prayer this week. I know that your mom is hoping to reduce the herd before winter so she can concentrate on getting the house ready for the spring market."

"Yes, she met with a real estate agent yesterday. You should see the list," Enid sighed. "I've hired some extra help for mom in the barn. Ruth Genung and the Larkes are both trading help for lessons. Ruth is even entering her first show this weekend."

"That's great. She's a sweet kid."

"How do you know them? They don't have property or animals."

"Not large animals but they do have a puppy. They brought him in for his shots last week."

Jacob finished cleaning up his equipment and closed the cover over the truck's box. "I have to go. No time for

Going Home

lunch today, unfortunately. I don't know when I'll have a spare moment for anything again. My uncle is taking quite a bit of time off. Seems he has a new relationship that he's fostering." Jacob winked at Enid.

"I'm glad the show is this weekend. I have enough to keep me busy in the barn all day. I feel like an intruder every time I go in the house. I never know what I'm walking into," Enid laughed. "JR is not impressed, let me tell you. He caught your uncle and my mom in an embrace and he started jumping up and down barking like a jealous lover. If Ted even sits beside my mom, JR jumps up in between them. He even growled at your uncle yesterday. That was the last straw."

At the mention of his name the cheeky Jack Russell appeared from the feed room. "I have to keep him with me now. You've been banned haven't you, JR?" The terrier whined and whimpered telling all within earshot of the unfair treatment the new couple were imposing on him.

"That's hilarious, E. JR, you poor soul." JR moved his protest over to Jacob and received scratches and rubs to spur on his announcements.

"I'll see you, E. Hopefully before Sunday. I'll try to make it to the show. I'd really like to see you ride. Uncle Ted came home last week quite impressed."

"That would be great, Jacob. See you then."

With no horses to ride and no lessons that day, Enid decided to give her tack a thorough cleaning, and spent the rest of the day surrounded by the familiar smell of leather cleaner and neatsfoot oil.

Thursday's pony club lessons went well. Enid designed a course that the kids rode as a hunter course and then as a jumper course. Enid challenged the D2's to make tight turns and to move the pace up during the jump-off stage. Kyle and David both loved it, while Ruth rode conservatively. Hillary and Amelia refused to make any change to how they rode. Enid didn't mind. She knew they would be taking their instruction from Mrs. Crooms the following day at the jump rounds.

Friday found Enid putting the finishing touches on the two geldings. She bathed them and trimmed their whiskers, bridle paths and fetlock hairs. She had worked on their manes all week and had thinned them to a length that would produce neat and even braids. Ede, Ada, Ruth and Leonora had taken Enid's lead and all the equines going to the show donned shiny coats. Friday after school they made their way to the Fair grounds. Enid drove Homestead Farms' three-horse angle haul trailer with Home Hunter, Homebody and Wild Bill. The two boarders traveled together in Ede's trailer. The others would meet them there in time for the jump rounds that Enid had signed her students up for.

The Fair Grounds were abuzz with activity. It seemed everyone was there at the same time. Enid spotted Mrs. Crooms and Bekah right away. Their stable colors were magenta and silver, hard to miss. Mrs. Crooms was in the middle of the warm-up ring, coaching students. There were four children on ponies trotting around.

The group from Homestead Farms unloaded their horses and tied them to the sides of the trailers. The Babcock and Wilson families had shared a trailer and were unloading as well. Ada and Harry were first up for the 2' Hunter rounds. Enid left Leonora and Ruth to supervise the horses. Wild Bill was old enough to know what was going on and stood quietly munching hay. Homebody had been around the show grounds before and, like everything else, took it in stride.

Going Home

Home Hunter seemed to be looking to his older brother for the lead and decided to follow suit. If Homebody and Wild Bill found nothing to be upset about then Home Hunter wouldn't waste the energy either. He settled for munching on the sweet hay that was tied in front of him. While Harry and Ada tacked up, Enid set off for the arena to see what the warm up course consisted of.

"Enid, Enid Taylor, it's so good to see you again. How's your mom?" Mrs. Crooms walked over, extending her hand.

"Hi, Mrs. Crooms, it's nice to see you again, too. Mom is doing better. She'll be here tomorrow, though she shouldn't be."

"How does a doctor expect a busy and vibrant person like your mom to just stay inside? As if that will help her heal faster than being outside in the fresh air." Mrs. Crooms looked at her watch. "Well, it's our turn to jump. Best of luck tomorrow."

She waved her students over and they entered the ring.

Good, thought Enid. She could watch a couple of rounds before she entered with Ada and Harry. She turned to see if the two were on their mounts yet. Enid was pleased to see them walking toward the warm-up ring. Ede was close by.

Enid noted that the first course was easy and predictable. The epitome of a hunter course: across the diagonal, down the long side, across the other diagonal and down the other long side. No surprises, traps or tricky distances, just lope around the arena and get over the jumps that blocked your path in style. Mrs. Crooms' students tackled the problem easily. Enid thought one of the girls was mounted on Pixie, Bekah's first pony. As she cantered around close to the rail Enid realized it had to be Pixie. No other pony had that particular white stripe down its face to end in three of the tiniest snips Enid ever saw on a muzzle.

Wow, Enid thought, *Pixie must be at least 25-years-old.* As she was standing there staring at Pixie she heard someone walk up and stand beside her.

"Recognize my pony?"

Enid looked over to see Bekah's beautiful chiseled face. Her deep sea-green eyes were set in porcelain skin and surrounded by dark hair.

"She looks exactly the same, Bekah. Where does the time go? It seems like yesterday you were trotting around on that pony and I was on Davy Crockett," Enid said wistfully.

"It seems to me that it was only yesterday that you beat me at this show in the 4'6" Jumpers. But that's not going to happen this year." Enid saw a smile cross Bekah's face. "I'm not going in the 4'6" Jumper's so you can't beat me," Bekah laughed.

"I'm not either! I will be relegated to the 3' Hunters and the 3'6" Jumpers. What are you riding? I thought maybe you would have Mighty Joe Young here."

"No, I left him in California. He and I are in the 4'9" division this year. I came home to show the sale horses for mom. I'll be in the 3' Hunters as well. I guess we can duke it out there."

Enid joined the laughter. "How the mighty have fallen. Hunters, ugh! That was always more Mally's game than ours."

"True, we all had our strengths. Yours certainly was cross-country. You know I don't think I ever congratulated you on getting your A rating or ever really told you how sorry I was for your loss." Bekah's wishes were genuine. Enid was at a loss for a response.

Going Home

"Thank you," was all that emerged. "But, hey, the 4'9" division is certainly getting up there. Do you live in California permanently now?"

"I have an open invitation to stay. The owner's son, James, has kind of asked me to marry him. I came home to make that decision. I don't know if I'm ready to get married or call California home."

Mrs. Crooms was finishing up with her 2' students. Enid said good-bye to Bekah and made her way to the warm-up ring to help Harry and Ada before their jump rounds. She found them cantering around the ring happily.

"Ede, how are they doing?"

"Oh, good. I made them trot for longer than they wanted but both the ponies are behaving themselves. Thanks so much for the pointers for Mr. Big. I'm glad I came out earlier and lunged him. It makes a huge difference."

"I'm glad it's working out. Well, we're up next for the jump rounds." Enid motioned to Ada and Harry. They slowed to a walk and exited the arena following Enid to the in gate.

"Okay here's the course. It should be no problem memorizing it. Remember tomorrow to come here early enough to learn the courses and to watch a few rounds to see how it is riding. Let's go in."

Digger and Mr. Big snorted at the flower boxes in front of the first vertical. Enid was glad the course designer had put them out for the jump rounds. It was generous to let the inexperienced riders and their mounts deal with it before they were riding for ribbons.

"Pick up the trot and go around the whole ring a couple times each direction before you canter." The ponies trotted off erratically but soon settled when they figured the flower boxes weren't in fact monsters lying in wait to pounce on unsuspecting ponies.

Ada and Harry both did well over the course. Mr. Big chipped in a few extra strides the first time through so Enid encouraged Ada to make the pony move out a bit better. Digger dug in and did his job with style. The more Enid saw the pony the better she liked him. Both kids enjoyed the jump rounds and left feeling more confident about the following day.

All too soon their time was up. They made their way back to the trailer. As none of Enid's students were jumping 2'3" there was a bit of a wait before Leonora, Kyle, David and Ruth did the 2'6" rounds.

Enid used the time to walk Home Hunter around, showing him the sites and sounds that were unfamiliar to his day-to-day environment. Apart from a few snorts, he followed Enid placidly around. She then tacked him up and lunged him. He let out a few good bucks releasing some pent up energy before he settled into his perfect daisy cutter canter. Enid caught Bekah's gaze out of the corner of her eye. Bekah walked over.

"E, is that the four-year-old you have advertised?"

Enid wasn't surprised that Bekah would know what was for sale at Homestead Farms. The Crooms had been competitors in the horse market for years. Mrs. Crooms imported Coco Puff, a Dutch Warmblood stallion, 10 years ago from Holland. He had been a leggy, dark bay yearling but Enid knew from the first glimpse that he was special. Sure enough he developed into a powerful and athletic stallion. Mrs. Crooms had two nice thoroughbred broodmares and started populating the Comox Valley with talented Hunters and Jumpers. Although Homestead Farms didn't stand a

Going Home

stallion and bred Queenie only every other year Bekah and Enid knew what was on the line each time they were set against each other in a jump off.

"Yes, Queenie really stamped this one. Who knew he would so live up to his name?"

"I shouldn't be telling you this but in California he would bring double what you have him advertised for. The barn I'm in is filled with the rich and famous willing to buy their child an instant star. That's what you have at the end of the lunge line, an instant star."

"You know my mom, she'll have to check out any potential owner for the 'permanence factor' over any dollar value. Actually someone from California is coming to see him and Homebody this weekend."

"Really… hmm," Bekah waved good-bye and went to find her mom.

Enid led the gray gelding back to the trailer. She settled him and then went to gather the riders for the 2'6 division. Everyone was excited to get their practice rounds in. Apart from Leonora feeling awkward riding with the kids, all went well. Joe hunkered down and did his job. Digger cantered around as if to tell all the other ponies that he had already cleared the arena from monsters and to follow him. Ruth was so confident and pretty in her rounds that Enid had high hopes for her tomorrow. David, aboard Charlie, needed reminding to use the whole arena and not to cut corners in a Hunter class. By the time Enid was done, Mrs. Crooms was waiting in the wings with Hillary, Amelia and two other girls on horses just as nice as Lilac and Dancer. It appeared that Mrs. Crooms wasn't yet moving Hillary to the 3' Division. But as this was the first show of the season, Enid wasn't surprised. After all, she didn't want to remain at the 3'6" level with Homebody anymore than Hillary wanted to stay at 2'6." Enid wished she could stick around and watch but Home Hunter needed as long a warm-up as possible.

When Enid entered the arena 45 minutes later on Home Hunter a small crowd, in tell tale magenta and silver jackets, had gathered on the bleachers to watch. *Great*, thought Enid, *an audience, just what I don't need*. Then again maybe it was an advantage to have people in the bleachers today.

The gray took longer to convince than the ponies that the infamous flower boxes were indeed inanimate objects. As he approached the first vertical it was a battle to keep him straight. When he conceded to jump, it was anything but hunter-like. Enid expected it and was in control to stop any playful buck, on the landing side. She circled the jumps until she recovered the geldings full attention then completed the course in true hunter style. She was pleased. If the gelding did as well tomorrow he would show his true potential to any interested party.

As she exited the arena she could hear the twittering rising from the silver and magenta crowd. Bekah came over to walk beside the sweating gelding. "E, he is spectacular."

"Thanks, Bek, but you know I've only been riding him for three weeks. Mally did most of the work."

"She did a good job starting him. And you'll do a great job showing him tomorrow. I'm not sitting on anything quite as pretty."

Bekah parted with E and made her way to the magenta trailer. Enid could see a gangly almost black mare tacked up and waiting impatiently, pawing the grass at her large feet. Enid knew she must be a Dutch Warmblood, as that's what the Crooms bred. Most of them are slower to develop and the mare was probably only three, therefore, she was

Going Home

excused her leggy disproportioned look. Again, Enid didn't have time to watch. She wanted to get on Homebody and go for a nice walk around the trails before she went into the warm-up ring.

Ede took over the cooling out of Home Hunter to free Enid's attention for Homebody. She was back in the saddle in record time. Ruth had Wild Bill groomed to a shine and was now working on her tack. Ada was sitting beside her with a pout, polishing away.

"Ada, why the face?" Enid asked.

"I wanted to watch you but Mom said I have to do everything she does." She pointed a soapy finger at Ruth. "Mom says I can learn a thing or two from her." Again she refused to mention Ruth's name. Ruth just kept on cleaning, ignoring the rudeness of the child next to her.

"You'll have plenty of time tomorrow to watch me but now is the best time to clean your tack." Enid received a glare from Ada, reserved for all who would unite against her. With a 'humph' she returned to the soap.

Enid enjoyed the trail ride as much as Homebody. Riding through the familiar woods, seeing the jumps tucked here and there between the trees gave Enid a chance to let all the emotions settle. It was weird to be back, carrying on as if she never left. Feeling the contained power under her walking placidly along just waiting for her to release it, to conquer gravity, made her wonder how she ever thought that anything she'd accomplished in her Vancouver career could compare. It was obvious to her now the difference between fulfillment and filling time. She didn't want to just fill in time anymore. She realized that it wasn't just Home Boy and her father she had lost that tragic day, she had walked away from, died to, her real self, her real purpose. She turned the gelding toward the warm-up ring and as he moved into his huge elastic trot, Enid smiled.

Chapter Twenty-Two

After the Homestead team returned from the schooling rounds they finished up a few last-minute chores. Ede, Ada, Leonora and Ruth all stayed to braid their horses. Enid enjoyed the camaraderie and kibitzing that flew around the barn like swallows on a summer evening. When she finally chased them all home, turned out the lights and headed up to the house, it was with a whistle on her lips and a skip in her step. She caught herself and laughed. She felt like a little kid anticipating Christmas morning. Excited and curious but not scared.

It was an empty house that Enid entered. Ted had taken Meredith out to the movies. It got her mom out of the house, and away from all the familiar pre-show activities. Although Meredith had made the decision to refocus her life, it was difficult to quit cold turkey. Good habits were just as hard to change as bad ones.

She opened the back door and took the boots off of her tired feet. She hung up her hoodie and went into the bathroom to wash up. As she looked in the mirror she barely recognized herself. Her hair was overgrown out of the uptown coif, there were smudges of dirt on her face, her cheeks were rosy from the outside air, and her eyes were sparkling with life. She washed up. Her nails were chipped and dirty, her hands stained with saddle oil. She was drained but she'd never felt so fulfilled. She left the dirty water to find its own way down the drain and went to the kitchen. After a quick supper of good old carbohydrates in the form of macaroni, and protein in the form of cheese, she picked up her coffee and went for her dad's chair. As she sat in the worn recliner she felt what she could only describe as a warm glow envelope her. She closed her eyes. She let tears stream down her face unchecked. There was no sorrow in them, neither joy. She breathed in and started to talk.

"Daddy, I'm sorry. I've been angry with you for so long for leaving me. I've been angry with a lot of people for abandoning me and today I realized that really, I was the one that truly walked away. Thanks for everything you did for me, for all of us. Thank you for being a Godly man, for always leading me to Jesus. I'm sorry I forgot, that I walked away from Jesus too.

"Jesus, I'm sorry. Father in Heaven, thank you that you never left me or abandoned me. Thank you for bringing me home, even when I didn't want to. You know what's best. Thanks for mom and Ted, bless them in their relationship. Help me to make decisions for my future. I need your wisdom." Enid kept her eyes closed. The tears subsided. She rested in the glow, in the warmth. Deep in her spirit she heard a deep velvety voice whisper her name.

"Enid, I love you. I have plans for you. I welcome you home. You are home."

Going Home

"Yes, Lord, yes, Jesus I am."

Enid didn't know how long she sat there, on her dad's chair, in the glow. She was shaken back to earth when the kitchen door burst open and two curly heads came bounding in.

"Auntie E, Auntie E!" Dina and Donny catapulted their tiny frames straight at Enid.

She grabbed them in a bear hug, burying her face in the curls.

"Dina, Donny! I am so glad to see you. Let me look at you." She let them go so that they could stand for inspection. "You must have grown 2 whole inches since Christmas!" They beamed with pride.

"They have. I can't keep any clothes in the closet long enough to fit them more than a few weeks."

"Liz," Enid stood and embraced her sister-in-law. Liz squeezed back.

"You look good. Congratulations on your new baby-to-be."

"Thanks E, you look great!" Liz smiled widely.

Mike came over to the women and took the spot over in front of his sister. They embraced warmly.

"It's good to see you, Mike."

"E, I'm sorry if I was a jerk. Forgive me?"

"Of course. I was no saint myself. Forgive me?"

"Of course."

The siblings smiled at each other then Enid punched Mike's arm playfully.

"Ow," he whined.

Donny and Dina jumped on their dad. "Dog pile!" Donny yelled.

Mike wrestled with his kids while Liz and Enid found the kettle.

"Better boil some water for hot chocolate," Liz said. "The twins have been waiting all day to drink it at grandma's. Seems it tastes the best here. By the way, where is Mom? Is she in bed already?"

Before Enid could answer the door swung open revealing a glowing Meredith and Ted.

"Mike, Liz, babies!" she cried.

"Grandma!" they came running over. Ted intercepted the whirling dervishes, scooping them up together.

"There you go, Donny and Dina. Now you can hug your grandma one at a time. We wouldn't want to knock her off the crutches, would we?"

The twins looked with big eyes into Ted's sparkling ones. They sensed the friendliness and quickly responded to him.

"No, I don't want grandma to get hurt again," said Donny.

"Me either," chirped in Dina.

Ted let them put their chubby arms around Meredith's neck one at a time. Meredith hugged back as best she could with the crutches under her arms.

"Okay, kids," Mike said, "Let Grandma sit down."

Ted put the kids down and they escorted Meredith to her rocker. They ran around trying to help her get settled. Dina gave her the doll she was carrying. Donny brought the stool over so grandma could put her feet up. The kettle whistled loudly in the kitchen.

"Why doesn't everyone sit down and Enid and I will bring the hot chocolate," Mike announced.

Enid knew what was coming... the third degree. As

they entered the kitchen Mike asked, "What's Dr. Brown doing with Mom?"

"What do you mean by that? He isn't 'doing anything' with mom, they're good friends. He's been a great help."

"They looked like more than friends to me," noted Mike.

"Would it be a problem for you if they were?"

"I don't know, I haven't thought about the possibility."

"Well, you should. You should also know that Mom is getting ready to sell Homestead Farms," Enid reached for the mugs and the powder.

Mike looked at her, trying to keep his chin off the ground. "You're kidding, right?"

"No, she's serious," Enid showed him the realtor's list of suggested fix-ups stuck on the fridge with a Tim Horton's magnet.

"Wow, I never thought I'd see the day. What gives, E?" Mike looked at her while stirring the warm liquid vigorously, "Is she that sick? Is there something she isn't telling us?"

"No, she'll be fine when she recovers. She's just ready to move on with her life the way dad and she talked about. Traveling, doing short-term mission trips, not being so tied to home." Enid put the drinks on a tray, adding a plate of homemade chocolate chip cookies.

"I know it's a bit of a shock but when she talks to you about it be happy for her. I am."

Enid carried the tray out to the waiting family. Mike stayed back for a moment to let all the news sink in and then joined the others in the family room.

Chapter Twenty-Three

Morning came early for Enid. After checking her email she left the house as quietly as possible. The adults had stayed up late talking. Ted had taken Mike outside for a while and when they came back there were broad smiles all around. It seemed that he must have asked Mike's permission to date his mom because upon returning Ted kissed Meredith sweetly on the lips for all to see. Liz was pleasantly surprised, while Meredith was embarrassed but happy. Ted was beaming and Mike joined his mom in the embarrassed corner. Enid sat back and laughed at them all, having already earned her get-out-of-jail free card from embarrassment.

Meredith talked openly about selling and Mike was supportive. Liz was surprised once more but being the gentle, giving person she was, she only wished Meredith to be happy. The entourage didn't need to be at the fair grounds before lunch, so Enid had wished them all a good night and had left the two couples laughing over the latest twin episodes.

As Enid approached the barn, she noticed that the lights were already on. Leonora's car was parked in front. "Hey, what do you think you're doing?" teased Enid. "I could have slept longer if I knew you were feeding."

"I couldn't sleep that's why I'm here so early. I'm so nervous."

"Well, you're doing the right thing with it. Working. Thanks for feeding."

"You're welcome," Leonora said. "Do you feel like throwing up, too?"

"No, not yet anyway!" laughed Enid. "Ask me again before I get on Home Hunter, especially with the family from California there."

"Did you hear from them?"

"Yes, they emailed to let me know that they would indeed be there. It seems the mysterious Californians are none other than the family that Bekah is working for. I wondered yesterday when she was talking to me about Home Hunter. She told me I had him under priced. Oh, well, we'll see what happens."

Enid showed Leonora how to take the neat long braids that she had finished last night and tie them up. Each braid ended up neatly folded and tied with yarn the same shade as the gelding's coat. Enid was just starting the two young geldings when the Larkes arrived with Ruth. Everyone finished about the same time. They loaded up the equines and headed for the fair grounds.

The morning went well. Enid was very pleased with how her students did. Ada and Harry both placed well in the 2' division. Mr. Big behaved himself for the most part. It took Ada two rounds to get her pace right so that the pony went around without chipping in extra strides. She won the

Going Home

last class. Digger was a star and Harry came away with two thirds and a second. Both the children were pleased and so were their families.

The Junior 2'6" division had the most entries. That was usual so Enid had her students sign up on the schedule board as a group. This enabled them to ride their three courses back to back without having to wait for the entire class to go. This also helped the riders by having an estimated time to enter the ring. The "open card" system was routinely used in the Hunter Jumper show circuit

David opted to be first from their group. His rounds were steady but he still rode them more like a jumper than a hunter. Enid didn't scold him too much because she recognized a bit of her own impatience in his approach to the Hunter ring. He went home with a 6th and a reserve. Kyle concentrated on his lines and Digger showed more style over the higher jumps. He ended up with three thirds. Ruth rode precisely and presented a pretty picture to the judges. Wild Bill loped around the course more like a gentleman than a gunslinger. The judge took notice and gave Ruth the Reserve Championship behind Hillary. Amelia rode around safely and was happy with her fourths and fifths.

In the senior version of the 2'6" Hunters, Leonora and Joe, or Bar Code, as the announcer called him, had three good rounds. Leonora made some nervous mistakes in the first class. Enid had her do some breathing exercises and then she settled down and rode the next rounds more efficiently. She came away with a fourth and a sixth. All in all, it was a good morning for the Homestead group. Everyone decided to get lunch during the 2'9" division.

After lunch Enid went to connect with the Californians before she had to get Home Hunter ready. She found them peering over his stall door. "Hi, you must be the Cellinis, I'm Enid Taylor." She extended her hand in a business-like manner.

"Enid, it's good to meet you. I'm George, this is my wife, Angelina, and my son James." They took turns greeting each other.

"And this must be Home Hunter." He gazed over the stall door appreciatively.

"Yes, and his brother, Homebody, is right next to him," Enid pointed out.

"Shall I take him out for you to see?" Enid reached for Home Hunter's halter.

"Please, if you have time," George replied.

"Sure, I'll get him out and then you can see him groomed and saddled." Enid began her routine as if at home alone. The Cellinis kept a polite distance, not interfering but watching. The gelding stood as good as gold. Enid knew he would behave himself. She had walked him already that morning and found that he had settled in like a trooper.

The Cellinis spoke quietly amongst themselves but Enid heard snatches of the comments, admiring Home Hunter's temperament and conformation. When the gray was tacked up, Enid slipped on his back expertly and led them to the warm-up ring. She joined the ranks already trotting and cantering around. Home Hunter bunched a bit in his back looking for an excuse to do things his way. Enid figured that included playfully bucking around so she immediately put him to trot in a smallish circle gradually expanding it and then shrinking it once more. She let the gelding trot straight only when the bump under the saddle had been replaced with the elastic swing that showed the gelding's true gait. After approximately 20 minutes of trotting, walking and cantering,

Going Home

she popped him over the two jumps set in the middle of the ring. He was a bit wild to begin with but settled into his beautiful stride. Bekah was up on the black filly trying to keep her mind on the job at hand. The filly was flinging her feet in every direction. She was sweet enough but so gawky it was comical. To the trained eye the future potential was there to see but to others she appeared as a black storm cloud being blown around the arena by an ill wind. The Cellinis had eyes only for Home Hunter.

Enid had Ede sign her up to go in first so at the end of her warm-up she walked to the in gate. The jump crew was making the final arrangements. Enid took the time to memorize the three different courses and to breathe.

When her number was called she entered the arena at the trot getting the gelding to yield to her legs and hands, keeping his mind on her. She trotted around the arena once then put Home Hunter into his world-class canter, and headed for the first line of fences. Home Hunter was primed and intent on the jumps. He over-jumped the first few before settling into the skimming efficiency top Hunters exhibit. Enid left the arena very proud of his accomplishment. As she exited she heard an eruption of applause in the stands. Her mom, Ted, Mike, Liz and the twins were all in their designated places. And to Enid's surprise, Jacob, Mally and Tim were among the crowd. She waved as Home Hunter placidly walked on a loose rein. She let him stand and watched as two other riders went. She then entered for the second round and felt the settled canter from the first stride. The gelding knew his job and executed it flawlessly. The third round was as good and Enid could not recall ever enjoying the Hunters as much. She dismounted the gray away from the in gate. As she was running the last stirrup up the leather, she saw James

Cellini approaching her. He was tall, dark, and dressed in tan breeches and shiny boots.

"May I ride him now, Miss Taylor?"

Enid reluctantly agreed. She felt the gelding had done enough but James Cellini had come a distance to see this horse. It was only right to let him ride.

He sensed her reluctance. "I won't tax him, Miss Taylor. I just want to see if he feels as good as he looks."

"Of course, I'm sorry." Enid handed him the reins.

James mounted proficiently. Home Hunter pricked his ears at the added weight but otherwise made no objections. James expertly and generously let the gelding walk out on a loose rein. He slowly picked up contact and headed for the warm-up ring. Enid was just about to call him back when she noticed a competitor number pinned to his back. No one was allowed in the ring except registered competitors. James asked the gelding to trot out and Home Hunter obeyed quietly. Enid could tell nothing from the poker straight look on James' face. He gave away his cards, though, when the gelding cantered. James looked over at his parents and raised his eyebrows letting the slightest smile escape his lips. True to his word, he brought the gray back to a walk and exited the arena after no more than a 5-minute ride. Enid was impressed with his ability and that he kept his word. James dismounted lightly and proceeded to loosen the girth and run the stirrups up the leathers.

"Thank you Miss Taylor," was all he said. He handed the reins back to her and walked to where his parents were. Enid turned the gelding and led him back to his stall. Jacob, Mally and Tim were waiting for her.

"E, you were great," Mally said giving Home Hunter a hug. "So were you, Gilligan." She planted a kiss on the big

Going Home

gelding's nose. He nickered quietly muzzling her pockets. "Okay, okay, don't be so impatient. I wouldn't come without a treat," Mally revealed the hidden treasure. Home Hunter munched contentedly on the sugar cubes.

"Gilligan?" queried Enid.

"He was so gawky as a three-year-old, I had to call him something. Gilligan stuck. It's been our little secret," Mally started to untack the gelding.

"It's okay, Mal I can do it," Enid protested.

"Please let me E, I've really missed him."

Enid conceded. Tim reached out to pat the gelding. "Like old times, E, except for the fact that it looked as if you actually enjoyed the Hunter Ring."

"On this guy it is a 'whole new world' as the song goes," Enid lovingly scratched behind the sweaty gray ears.

"My uncle didn't exaggerate. You ride beautifully, E."

"Thanks, Jacob. It's amazing what a couple weeks back in the saddle can accomplish."

"So who's the guy?" Tim asked.

"James Cellini, he's the son of the family that Bekah is working for in California. They're here on a buying trip."

Enid noticed the furtive glance between Mally and Tim. Before she could say anything, the twins were upon her. "Auntie E you're a star!" Dina announced.

"Yeah, Auntie E, a star," Donny added.

"Great job, sis," Mike added his pat to Home Hunter's warm neck.

"Pick me up Daddy, I want to pat the horse," Donny cried.

"No, me first Daddy," whined Dina.

Mike picked them both up and Home Hunter soaked up the attention like a love-starved puppy dog. Enid noticed her mom hobbling towards her. Ted was close in case she placed a foot wrong. Enid met her half way.

"E, you've done wonders with that horse. He was marvelous."

"Thanks Mom, but it was Mally who laid a great foundation in his early training. Anyone could have gotten on him. He made me look good."

"Yes, Mally is really good at starting young horses."

"She looked a bit upset when I mentioned the Cellinis were looking at Home Hunter."

"She loves that horse. Ever since Bo Jangles died a couple of years ago she hasn't thought of owning another horse except Gilligan."

"You knew about Gilligan? I just found out!"

"I heard her talking to him all the time. I didn't want to intrude in their little secret. He's part of the reason she quit coming over to help. It was painful for her to think of him being sold. Unfortunately she knew more than anyone that I needed the money." Her mom changed the subject, "You'd better get ready for the 3'6" Hunters. There are only 2 entries in the 3'3" section."

"They were just finishing up the 3' Division so the results will be out soon. Your mom and I will go collect your ribbons," Dr. Brown said confidently.

"Okay, I'll see you later," Enid turned back to the stall area.

Mally had Home Hunter untacked, groomed and settled into a clean stall with fresh hay and water. It was great to have such expert help. Enid smiled as she watched her friend begin to groom Homebody, readying him for the saddle and bridle.

"Watch out or you'll get on steady," Enid teased.

Going Home

"I already warned you I'd be back," bantered Mally. "I'm certainly able to do more than help with feeding," she quickly stuck her tongue out at Tim as she continued grooming the gelding's dark coat, coaxing even more of a shine out of it. "You've done wonders on their appearance, E. I'm afraid when I left they were a bit scraggly."

"Most horses look like that coming out of winter, it's okay."

Enid turned to Jacob who seemed to not know what to do with himself, "Could you change my number, please?"

"Sure," he answered, happy to be of some use. He took the number she had taken off and switched the yarn to the next one. Every horse and rider combination required a separate number.

"737," noted Jacob, "You should be able to really fly with a number like that."

"I see the Brown sense of humor is in your genetic make-up," laughed Tim.

Enid was just getting a leg up when James Cellini walked over. "Congratulations on the Championship, Miss Taylor."

"Thank you, I never actually heard the announcement."

"I don't think there was any doubt, surely. Nothing up here compares to that gelding. Bekah's black may fill out decently in a year or two, but she's still not in his class. Surely you know that?"

"I never count my ribbons until they're on the board, Mr. Cellini." Enid paused, "May I introduce you to Mally and Tim Lewes, James Cellini. Mally started the gelding. I merely took over the riding duties 3 weeks ago. And Dr. Jacob Brown, James Cellini."

James politely shook everyone's outstretched hands.

"Mr. Cellini," started Mally.

"James, please," he protested.

"James, are you here buying for yourself or do you find horses for clients back home?"

"Both. I prefer riding in the jumper ring myself, however, our barn is filled with celebrity offspring and their parents prefer them to start in the Hunters. I quite agree. But they're a competitive lot and they like to win. I happen to have the knowledge and experience to make horse finding easy for them and worthwhile for my pocket book."

"I see, so you are, in essence, a horse dealer."

Enid heard the edge on Mally's voice. *She sounds like my mother*, was Enid's first thought. *She's going to blow the deal* was the second.

"If you want to use that crude out dated description. I am known as an Equine Appraiser in most circles. And a good one at that."

He turned his attention to Enid astride the big gelding. "I'm looking forward to seeing this guy go. I know the Hunters is not his forte however, I can wait until tomorrow to see him tackle the jumper ring. Have a good ride." And with that he was gone.

"Horse dealer," muttered Mally.

Enid decided this was not the time to discuss the differences of terminology or the inappropriateness of Mally's interference. She had three courses left to complete her day before it all happened again tomorrow in the Jumpers.

As she approached the warm-up ring, Enid was thankful the courses for 3'6" Division were the same as for the 3' Division; one less thing to worry about. James was standing with Bekah at the rail. He had his arm possessively around her shoulders. She looked uncomfortable. Enid looked away and finished popping Homebody over warm-up jumps trying

Going Home

to place him at a spot in front of the fence to minimize his ejection seat take off. No matter where he jumped from, the power was there. Enid made her way to the in gate as calmly as possible.

Her three rounds went smoothly. Not pretty enough to beat Mrs. Crooms on her stallion, Coco Puff, but the Reserve Championship was an unexpected bonus to the day's winnings for Homestead Farms.

Ede, Ada, Ruth and Leonora cheered loudly from one end of the ring while Enid's family and friends, minus Jacob, echoed the hoots from the other side. Mally was waiting at the gate with a cooler to throw over Homebody's back so he didn't get a chill. Enid dismounted and they led the gelding back to a clean stall. Home Hunter and Wild Bill were eating hay contentedly in their spotless homes away from home.

"Mally, you've done too much, Tim's going to be mad at me."

"No he won't and I didn't do it. Ada and Ruth are the stable elves you're looking for. Ede told me of the arrangements you made by trading for extra help. That's great. With that in place I should have no trouble replacing you when you return to Vancouver in three weeks. Leonora is willing to feed some mornings so it should be fine."

"Oh, that's great," Enid didn't know what to say. She hadn't thought of returning to the city in a while. She'd been so busy.

Mike, Liz, the twins, Meredith and Ted showed up.

"Hey, sis, we're heading home. Great day. Congratulations."

"Thanks, Mike. Thanks kids. See you at home."

The twins had picked some wild flowers and presented them to Enid. "Bye Auntie E," they replied in unison.

Meredith hugged her youngest child. "Thanks E, we'll talk at home about Home Hunter. I had a chat with the Cellinis and another prospective purchaser." Then she whispered just for Enid to hear, "Great job today, your dad would be so proud to see you riding again."

Enid squeezed her mom and then they were all off as fast as the twins could go with Ted's ever-watchful eye on Meredith.

"Where did Jacob run off to?" Enid asked.

"He had an emergency call," Mally replied. She looked at her friend, "Vets never sleep or have any kind of normal schedule. It's not the life for everyone that's for sure."

"You should know, Mally," laughed Enid.

They were just finishing up with Homebody, settling him for the night, when James and Bekah walked up. "Miss Taylor, may I have a word with you?"

Enid looked over at Mally, who slipped into Homebody's stall. "Sure."

"I'm a bit confused. You advertised the horses on the web yet I'm to understand your mother is the owner, is that correct?"

"Yes," Enid said unsure about where this was going.

"Do you have the authority to sell the animals or not?"

"No, I can't sell any of the horses without my mom's approval. She's funny that way. She likes to know what kind of home she's giving her babies to."

"Enid, really, horses are a commodity. Commodities are bought and sold all the time, sometimes for a profit and, unfortunately, sometimes for a loss. I'm offering your mom more than you advertised the horse for. You better talk some sense into her. I only have until tomorrow night and then I and my deep pocketed clients, are gone."

Going Home

"I will talk to my mom tonight, James. However, I could talk sense into my mom where her horses are concerned about as easily as you could convince one of your celebrity clients not to get the latest beauty treatment," Enid put on her negotiating persona. "She's the sole owner and will make the decisions accordingly."

James knew finality when he heard it. Bekah, who had looked sheepish until then flashed Enid a brilliant smile behind James' back and winked at her. It was all Enid could do to not burst out laughing.

"We'll talk tomorrow then?" James asked.

"Till tomorrow, Mr. Cellini," Enid shook his outstretched hand firmly.

Enid loaded up Home Hunter as he was not jumping tomorrow. Then, with Mally's help, they bedded Homebody down for the night and checked, unnecessarily, on Wild Bill. The efficient and thoughtful Ruth had already left with her proud parents. Mr. Big and Joe were at home by now in their own stalls.

Enid turned to Mally but, before she could say anything, Mally lifted up her hand. "E, I know I stepped over the line today with that James guy. I'm sorry."

"Actually, I was going to say thanks for all your help. It was great having you in my corner today."

"Really, you're not mad?"

"No, you got to say the things I couldn't. It'll all work out. I'm not worried. But if my mom did get another offer I'll be surprised." Enid looked at her watch. "I should go before Ede, Ada and Leonora do everything. I'll see you two later for dinner, right?"

Tim walked up just as Enid was jumping into the cab of

the truck. "We'll be there. We wouldn't want to miss it," Tim said enthusiastically.

Enid waved at the couple as she drove off with Home Hunter safely inside wrapped in his winning cooler.

The Taylor household, united with the Browns, minus Jacob who was still busy with lambing season, enjoyed a celebration dinner. Toasts were made to Liz and Mike on the expectation of their next child; Home Hunter earned praise for his first place efforts; Enid was toasted for the success of her students and her successful hunter rounds on Homebody. When there was a lull in the cheers and glass tinkling, Mike stood up. He cleared his throat.

"Excuse me but I would like to make a toast." All eyes were fixed on him. "I would like to toast Ted and my mom." Everyone looked at the older couple.

"Last night I was asked if it would be okay for Dr. Brown, Ted, to have my mom's hand in marriage. I agreed wholeheartedly. Congratulations."

There were hoops and hollers, tears and laughter, and then to everyone's amazement Dr. Brown got down on one knee. Holding open a ring box shimmering in 2-carat glory, he asked Meredith, in the presence of their children and grandchildren, to be his wife. Meredith tearfully put the glimmering diamond proudly on her vacant left hand.

After the excitement quieted down, Enid snuck into the kitchen to make coffee. Meredith followed her on crutches. "Enid I need to talk to you about Home Hunter."

"Mom, surely it can wait. This is a big night we don't need to talk about it now."

"But we do," Meredith looked serious enough for Enid to put the coffee down.

"The other offer is from Ted."

Going Home

"What? Why? What do you mean?" Enid was confused. What would Dr. Brown do with the horse? The obvious answer was missing in her mind. So much had happened in the last 24 hours; her mind was too full to deduce the simplest clues.

"He wants to buy Home Hunter for Mally," Meredith explained. Enid's mind clicked into gear.

"He's willing to write off our vet bill in exchange for the horse's papers. I agreed. I'm sorry about the Cellinis but I'm not sure I want my babies in California. It's hard enough when I sell them to Alberta."

"Mom, he's yours. You can sell him to any one you want to for however much you want. Mally will be thrilled," Enid gasped, "This calls for another toast! Come on."

The two Taylor women returned to the dining room. "Okay, now I have a toast," Meredith announced. Everyone stopped talking and looked at the woman on crutches.

"Congratulations are in order to me for selling Home Hunter." Everyone clapped and cheered, though Enid saw the crestfallen look on Mally's face.

"Yes, I had to negotiate a tough deal and as you all know I am a tough sell." Everyone laughed. Meredith always gave more than she took.

"So it's my great pleasure to say," she raised her glass, "Congratulations Mally, Giligan is all yours."

Mally's eyes grew wide, her mouth opened. "What do you mean, mine? I thought the Cellinis…"

"I couldn't let Giligan go to California, honey. I bought him for you."

"Daddy!" was all she said before the tears rushed out of her eyes. She turned to Tim. He enveloped her in his arms and held her till she composed herself. Mally then got up and embraced her dad and Meredith. Everyone was misty eyed by then.

"Mal," Tim said tenderly, "Let's go see your boy." Mally and Tim left the table for the kitchen door.

"Hey, turn the lights out when you're done," Enid called cheerily. "Now, who wants coffee?"

Chapter Twenty-Four

Sunday dawned with a threat of rain. It was hard for Enid to get up. It seemed so anticlimactic. Although Enid hadn't done much to promote the business side of Homestead Farms because of the unsure future, now with her mom engaged and the vet bill paid off, the immediate crunch was eased. But this gray morning Enid felt her future was the more unsure of the lot. If she was having a hard time picturing herself in her condo, in her office, in city clothes, she was having a harder time seeing anyone else riding Homebody, teaching her students, or being there for Mally. With gloomy introspection she arrived at the barn. She fed and then drove to the fairgrounds to take care of Homebody and Wild Bill. A frantic Ruth met her at the gate.

"Enid, he's gone, he's gone!" Ruth cried incoherently.

"Slow down, Ruth, who's gone?" Enid asked anxiously.

"Homebody, he's not in his stall." She was shaking. Shannon, Ruth's mom, jogged over to the truck.

"Ruthie, Enid, I think we found him."

"Climb in," Enid commanded. Shannon and Ruth scrambled into the cab. Enid drove to the stalls. Sure enough, Homebody's door was open, revealing the emptiness.

"Over here," Shannon called. She was out of the truck before it stopped and was jogging to the aisle one over from where they were stabled. Enid and Ruth followed close on her heels. There was Homebody, tied up looking bedraggled and forlorn. A girl of about 14 came over to Enid.

"I got here first this morning because my mare will colic if anyone eats before her. I saw this horse trotting around so I tied him up. Is he yours?"

"Yes, he's mine," Enid confessed.

"Good thing the gate is closed every night. He could have got on the road."

"Thank you so much for catching him," Enid said.

"You're welcome," the girl beamed.

"I'm Enid Taylor, this is Ruth and her mom, Shannon. What's your name?"

"I'm Kandy Banks. My mom is over there by my horse, Araminty."

Enid saw a slight blond woman standing over a piebald mare voraciously snatching hay out of a net. "Well, thank you again. I'll return your halter."

Enid led Homebody back to his side of the stall complex. She put him in his stall and immediately started to sponge him down and brush out his tail. He quietly munched his breakfast. Ruth began to get Wild Bill groomed for his morning class. The jumpers started at 2'6" so they were first up this morning. Shannon went for coffee. Kyle and David arrived a bit later and set to work grooming and saddling up. It appeared that they had hired Ruth to feed their ponies that morning. Enid smiled, remembering all the times she

Going Home

and Mally were hoodwinked into taking care of Tim's early morning chores. She wondered if that still happened in the Lewes residence.

Homebody was securely locked in his stall when Enid accompanied the three D2's to the warm-up ring. She watched as they walked, trotted and cantered the ponies. She was pleased to see each of them incorporate some lateral movements into the routine. She set a cross bar at the vertical jump and had them each trot over it. The ponies all seemed fresh and eager to jump. She gradually made the warm up vertical and oxer to the maximum height and width of 2'6." David had a stop at the spread fence. He tipped his shoulder forward when he approached the oxer. Charlie simply put on the brakes for once and decided that he wouldn't jump with David's weight over his front feet. Enid was glad it happened in the warm up ring. It was a good reminder for David to ride properly.

They were in the first group to go. Ruth volunteered to lead the group. She rode the course much like she rode the hunters the other day and while she was clean her time was slow. The first class was a simple speed class. Fastest one around with the least amount of faults won. David went next and tore around the arena knocking 7 whole seconds off of Ruth's time. Kyle tried to match David's speed but couldn't cut the corners quite as easily and while he was still clear he was two seconds off the pace. At the end of the division it was David walking his pony around proudly displaying the championship cooler while Hillary accepted the reserve. Amelia, Ruth and Kyle each came away with some ribbons and big smiles.

Enid watched Kandy jump the 3' Jumpers. She was wild and wooly but she sat naturally and Araminty was a black

201

and white catapult under her. Their mistakes were merely from inexperience. Enid wondered who their instructor was. She hadn't noticed anyone in the arena warming them up. She went and introduced herself to Mrs. Banks and found out that they had recently moved into the area and hadn't yet found an instructor. Enid explained where Homestead Farms was and told her about Pony Club. Mrs. Banks was grateful and took Enid's number. While Enid was finishing up talking to Mrs. Banks, Bekah walked over.

"Enid, do you have a moment?"

Enid said good-bye to Mrs. Banks and turned to Bekah. "Sure, how are you this morning?"

"Tired, I never slept a wink last night. Life can get complicated so fast. When I was in California this last year and a half I thought I had finally found what I wanted. Big shows, big prizes, rich people. But the thought of marrying James and being there long term surrounded by all the glitz, glamour and gluttony, I just can't do it. Coming home has been the best thing I've done in a long time. Man, I couldn't wait to get out of here but now I see that we have something special in the Comox Valley," Bekah took a deep breath.

"What I came here to tell you is that James and his parents left early this morning. I guess when I told them that I wasn't returning to California they saw no reason to stay. I'm sorry if I messed up your deal with Home Hunter or Homebody. I should have waited to tell them till tonight."

"It's okay. My mom sold Home Hunter last night. I don't think any of the Homestead Farms horses were heading to California so you didn't mess anything up. I've been doing some soul searching too. I left for all the wrong reasons. Now I don't know what to do. It's like I'm caught in the 'wood between the worlds' and I don't have a magic ring to direct

Going Home

me. I don't really have a home here, Mom is selling, and I'm having a hard time seeing myself in Vancouver. I don't know what I'm going to do."

"Why you don't sell whatever you have in Vancouver and buy your mom out. That's what I'm doing. I'll only be able to give her about half the value but my parents are happy about sharing the house with me as long as I take over the business side of things. I don't have anything to sell except my horse. He's half-leased right now to one of the nicest 'Hollywood' families. They offered to buy him numerous times for a ridiculous amount. I phoned them this morning. They're sending me a check. So, I have no reason to return to California. Mom is looking to retirement. My dad is finished at the school board next year. It just makes sense. This is what I love to do and I feel that this really is home after all."

Bekah wished Enid luck in the jumpers and went to find her mom. It seemed that she would now ride Coco Puff since James Cellini had left. Enid didn't have time to sit down and think about anything Bekah had talked about. She headed for the stall area.

Jacob surprised Enid by showing up just before her class.

"I thought you would be in church," Enid said.

"I got home about 3:00 a.m. I never woke up till 10:30. What time is it anyway?" He looked at his watch. It was 11:30 a.m. "You never rode till the afternoon yesterday. Why so early?"

"Not as many people in the Jumpers and since it's not on grass yet it doesn't draw as many entries. Later this summer there'll be quite a few more horses which means stiffer competition."

Enid asked for a leg up. Jacob skillfully complied. "Did you hear the news?"

"I heard quite a bit of news. One of us is out of a house that's for sure!" he laughed, "I'm not living with the newlyweds!"

Enid joined in the laughter welcoming the release of tension. "Let's talk later, I may even let you take me out for lunch or if I win I'll take you out."

"Deal."

Jacob walked over to find some coffee while Enid entered the warm-up ring. Homebody showed no signs of stiffness or soreness from his midnight romp. He was eager to work and Enid once more reveled in his powerful fluid stride. He popped over the jumps effortlessly. Bekah was having fun on her mom's stallion. Coco Puff had power, speed and cruise control. Enid had never seen Mrs. Crooms jump him higher than 3'6" but wondered with Bekah now in the jockey's seat, if they weren't going to have that rematch in the 4'6" Jumpers sooner than they thought.

There were only four entries in the 3'6" division. Enid opted to go first. She considered this show as a training experience for Homebody and herself and didn't want to get sucked into compromising her long-term goals for ribbons. Dwelling on this thought, she rode very conservatively in the speed class. She was clear but fourth. Bekah smoked all the competition winning by three seconds.

The next class had an immediate jump off so Enid kept two courses in her mind while she entered the arena. She decided she could ask the gelding to go a bit faster and tighter. She went double clear and had a very fast time in the jump off. She exited smiling. Bekah caught her eye and smiled back. She tried to ride the same tight line that Enid

Going Home

etched in the sand but it cost her a rail as the stallion got too close to the last vertical. Enid went from fourth to first.

The last class saw Enid and Bekah with rails in the combination. The second of the three jumps had a blue plastic pool under it filled with water. Enid hadn't thought of schooling with a liverpool at home. Although Homebody had jumped the water fences last year, he still wasn't convinced that they were safe. He over jumped it so much that he couldn't negotiate the last fence clearly. Coco Puff felt the same way about liverpools. They harbored sea monsters.

Bekah left the arena laughing, "I forgot how much he hates liverpools."

"I forgot all about liverpools!" replied Enid.

Home Boy had had no problem with water of any kind after Enid had gotten over the initial training. She was sure Homebody would be the same. The championship ended up going to the only man in the class riding a big Belgian cross mare. Bekah ended up as Reserve.

"Congratulations, Bekah," Enid offered congenially.

"Thanks, I suppose we'll be meeting each other often in the Jumper ring again?"

"I don't know. I have some major decisions to make. It was really great to see you again. And good luck with your business."

Enid walked the gelding back to the stall. Ede and Ada had come to watch the jumpers and, together with Ruth, they had everything ready to go. They even had Homebody's stall stripped of all the shavings leaving it clean for the next show.

"You three are spoiling me. Thanks," Enid said.

"No problem, E, glad to help. Tough luck in that last class." Ede remarked.

"No such thing as luck. I never prepared for liverpools. My oversight."

"I guess that means I'm buying lunch," Jacob called out as he walked over.

"Guess so," Enid said as she slipped off the gelding.

"Is there anything I can do to help?" Jacob asked.

"No, thanks. I think we have it handled."

"Well, in that case, I'll meet you at the Whitespot."

"Okay, see you there." Enid continued walking the gelding toward the stall area. Homebody wasn't too hot after his efforts in the jumper ring. It only took about twenty minutes to untack him and cool him down enough to load him up for the trip home. With the help of Ede, Ada, and Ruth they were heading home in no time.

Once there, the girls settled the horses back in their regular stalls and then displayed the ribbons proudly in the tack room. Enid thanked her barn buddies for all their help and then left them to meet Jacob at the Whitespot for lunch.

She had changed her breeches and boots for jeans and sneakers. Her hair was tied back in a ponytail. She wore no make up. On the drive over she thought about everything that had happened the last few weeks. She heard the observations vocalized by Bekah reverberating in her head. She felt the same but could she do it? Should she do it? Maybe the answer was as simple as buying Homebody from her mom and moving him to Vancouver. She could continue with her job and add horses back into her life. She was weighing the pros and cons in her mind and just about missed the turn into the Whitespot.

Jacob was waiting in the foyer for her. "Hi, have you been waiting long?"

Going Home

"No, I just got here. I figured you had some stuff to do at the barn and would probably want to change."

"You figured right. I hope you're always so astute. I need to ask you for some advice."

Enid knew that Jacob didn't believe in coincidences. He was sold out on the sovereignty of God. It colored every aspect of his perception. That's why Enid felt she should talk to him.

The greeter came and seated them in a booth by a window. Enid looked at the funky pictures and felt a sense of home. Her dad used to bring her out to breakfast at least once a month and it was always here.

The waitress brought coffee and informed them that breakfast was still being served since it was Sunday. Enid ordered the Eggs Benedict and Jacob decided on steak and eggs. They chatted about Ted and Meredith, wondering how the announcement went at church. Jacob shared in the excitement for the upcoming wedding and for Mally's future with Home Hunter. When she was finishing up her eggs, she casually mentioned what Bekah's plans were. How she was investing in her mom's business and taking over the day-to-day operations.

Jacob looked up from his steak. "Are you thinking of doing the same thing, E?"

"I don't know, I just don't know. It's been so great to be home, to teach again, and to ride again. Homebody is everything I dreamed he would be. I just don't know. It would be easier to buy him from my mom and move him to Vancouver than to quit my job, sell my condo and move back here to what? Hard work and little pay. I just don't know." She looked at Jacob searching his eyes for answers. He had helped her so much since she met him. She was hoping that once more he would speak wisdom to her.

"E, you have to make the decision. The road is clearly set before you. One way may not be better or worse. God can use you and help you grow in your faith no matter where you are. I guess the question is where do you want to be in one year, five years, or twenty years? What do you want out of life? If you get married and have children what kind of home and family-life do you value? There are a lot of variables to consider. No one can make the decision for you. It sounds like Bekah came to an understanding more about herself than about the Cellinis. She didn't want to be surrounded and sucked in to what she saw in California as the measuring stick of success. Her world became smaller but richer because here is where she feels at home, at peace.

"I could have easily stayed in Southern Ontario and had a very successful vet practice. I had to leave home to find it. Uncle Ted's offering is a chance that very few vets my age are given. I'm truly blessed. And with his upcoming marriage and retirement not too far off I know that I'm in the right place at the right time. God knew I needed to move on. He led me here and I'm so glad to have found family and friends." Jacob took her hand and squeezed it.

"I'm glad I met you too, Jacob. It's been really helpful to have a friend to bounce things off of. Besides that you're a very valuable Scrabble partner." They laughed together. "I know I have to make this decision on my own. Thanks for listening."

Enid drove home with many thoughts and scenarios running through her mind. She pulled in just as Ted was pulling out. They waved at each other. She knew she would never call him dad, and he wouldn't expect it, however she

Going Home

realized that if and when she ever did have children they would have the same grandpa as Mally's kids. That was too cool.

Meredith was alone in the kitchen when Enid came in. "Hi, mom, where's Mike and Liz?"

"Oh, they took the twins up to Mt. Washington. How did you do today?"

"I rode like Mally in the first class and was clear but last. Then I pulled out all the stops and won the next one. In the last class the triple combination had a liverpool. He over jumped it and we had a rail coming out over the last vertical. I still felt really good about it and hope to move him up to the 4' division by the end of the summer." Enid heard herself making the long-term plans for Homebody. Her mom noticed too but didn't point it out. She was waiting for Enid.

"And how did the D2's do?" Meredith asked instead.

"David is great! He reminds me so much of Tim. He won the 2'6" Jumper championship. Hillary was reserve. No one was beating Charlie pony today. Boy can he speed. I don't think he's limited to the 2'6" range. I bet he could compete at the three foots. I've been thinking of ways to keep the kids interested into the C levels. Ruth is limited by the lack of her own horse but I think we made progress with having her help out here. She can get more riding in and earn some money for shows. Kyle might be the hardest one to convince to keep in pony club but I've been looking into Tetrathalon. It has running, swimming, shooting and riding. Interest is growing in tetrathalon here on the Island and clubs have sent members to national and international competitions. That might appeal to the boys and we're lucky enough to have boys. Oh, I also met a new girl named Kandy

Banks. She rode the 3' Jumpers on a cute piebald mare. I talked to her mom and they're going to phone this week to set up lessons and think about pony club. I bet she could test her D2 right away."

Again Enid heard the long term plans. She looked around the familiar room. Surrounding her were memories, history, purpose, a future. She took a deep breath and looked her mom in the eyes. Meredith was smiling benignly back at her.

"Mom, I've been thinking. I'm not sure what your plans are with Ted but since you're selling Homestead Farms anyway, what would you say if I offered to buy it from you?"

Meredith broke into a smile that could have lit a room up in the middle of winter. "I would say welcome home baby, welcome home."

∼ The End

TATE PUBLISHING & *Enterprises*

Tate Publishing is committed to excellence in the publishing industry. Our staff of highly trained professionals, including editors, graphic designers, and marketing personnel, work together to produce the very finest books available. The company reflects the philosophy established by the founders, based on Psalms 68:11,

"THE LORD GAVE THE WORD AND GREAT WAS THE COMPANY OF THOSE WHO PUBLISHED IT."

If you would like further information, please call
1.888.361.9473
or visit our website
www.tatepublishing.com

TATE PUBLISHING & *Enterprises*, LLC
127 E. Trade Center Terrace
Mustang, Oklahoma 73064 USA